SAVAGE RECREATION

Books by Ian Bloom

SCREWDRIVER
SAVAGE RECREATION

Savage Recreation

Ian Bloom

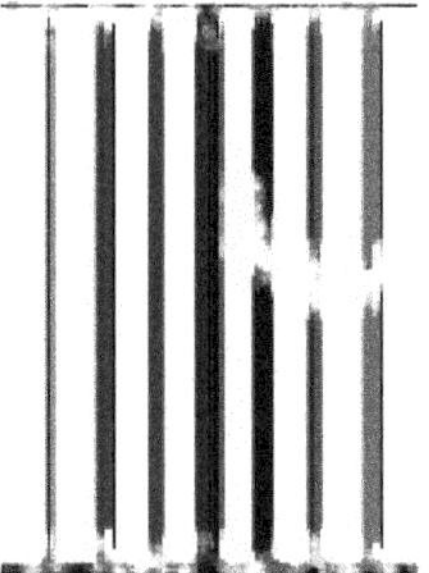

IAN BLOOM

Ian Bloom is an American art dealer and founder of Natural Gallery.

SAVAGE RECREATION

Contents

Fresh Taste

There's a plague. It's all around us. Akin to some miasma that is so constant that it's normal register. Cigarette smoke helps me forget. Perfume has the opposite effect. I'm reminded of the plague's lingering presence in the summer most. The heat awakens heathen scum to emerge from their coffins and feed. Some only make it to the corner, or end up in a jailcell. Either way, they do it all over again the next day.

I've had a preoccupation with geriatrics. I stare at my hands, my feet, vascular pipes, see my nails grow. It's simply that I'm dying. It's normal—becoming a corpse. I have scars that never fade. I don't mind those too much. The uvula, that thing hanging in the back of your mouth—mine looks larger, even swollen. My teeth seem to have sunk back into my mandible. Or is it that my jaw has just crept outward so there's more space between my teeth and my lip-mouth region. I don't fucking know, but I'm certain there's more deadspace. My tongue has more room to roam around. My nose doesn't seem to work as well as it used to. Maybe it's just the cigarettes. My shoulders crack if I extend my arms in a circular motion. That never used to happen. One day, are they just going to buckle and I'm going to be some gimp arm schmo? I don't know. Toil for no reason. I'll have a beer, instead. Scratch my balls. Wash my face.

Back to the plague, the rotting decadence, the city denizens have been scoured. It's either an internal devolutionary process that has come to fruition or it is an external reaction to the lack of stewardship the human race has displayed ad infinitum. I assume it's a combination of both. Some endless cycle. Like the true motion of the planets in our galaxy. That model they show you in grade school, with the sun in the middle, and all the planets in our solar system attached to rods to hold them in place. It's hogwash. Planets don't just move. I mean, they do, but the entire solar system is moving through space, too. It's a light show from a rave with the light wielding raver wholly moving perpetual at the same time. Deductive reasoning should hold true. Everything can be applied to that reality, relatively thinking.

Maybe it is a good thing that everything's burning. I prefer it rather than a torrential storm or massive flood to reset the status quo. When there are fires, it's a spectacle. Out in true American country, like Wyoming, they just let fires burn out without intervention. Human affairs would probably be better if we let them sort themselves out. On a microcosmic scale, of course, Street justice. There's no such thing as the Justice League. If there were Nietzschean supermen out there, then maybe there could be an argument for the moral obligation to be applied. Overall, the ones that play that role are impostors, dilettantes, charlatans. Anyway, I tend to underestimate the stupidity of others, and it's been a problem.

Now, back in mid May, the sirens were blaring in the streets erratically, like they'd start, then stop suddenly, only to start up again and then stop, and so forth, like three-shot Garand bursts. Was the cop just fucking with whoever he so desired to pursue, or not pursue? It seemed like it. I was in the backseat, cuffed, and when he had so conscientiously tucked my head down into the car, I noticed a box of donut excrements littered across the front. Fucking pig. He had to feed his rotten soul and what better than to disturb others for his viewing pleasure. To hell with they see the worst asshole of the social sphere. You sign up, you make your bed. So deal with it. Proper. Your definition.

This was on Grand Street and we had crossed into Chinatown. Most of the time, if not all of the time, the Chinamen do not give a shit if you are not one of them. Anything that can transpire on their streets is exempt from observation, care, or desire, if it's not Chinese. So now, I noticed the old timers smoking and getting agitated by the cop's foolish abuse of power. It started to worry me. Had something broken in the system?

The pig's lewd sirens sputtered on and off and when we hit Clinton Street, he veered down the hill towards the bridge, and drove passed the station. He kept going East and when we reached Columbia Street, he turned towards the projects. He parked his car under the bridge, before the projects, and took out a sharpie marker and wrote something on the back of my shirt. I assumed the first word was Kill because I noticed he had written two L's and the word was short. The other word, I assumed had to be riot ensuing. He threw me out of the car, and left me to fester. Soon enough, some high school kids started pestering me, so I remained calm. In two minutes, I was severely beaten to a pulp. No questions, no trial, just punishment. I took off the shirt as I stumbled east onto the walkway over the expressway. Said Kill Niggers—I guess I had committed a crime.

My thoughts weren't bitter or angry. Just standard callous silence. I made it to the amphitheatre in the East River Park and soaked in the shade of the trees. When I awoke, the blood had dried and crusted over above my eye. There were squiggly lines of red from my hands down to my elbows. A kid was pissing in the water fountain and he ran away when he saw me coming. I tried to refresh myself with the water and it didn't do much for me.

Ritual Obsidian

There was a cool breeze that passed through the archway. It carried to the vantage point overlooking the dunes. The leaves bristled in subtle waves until they fell free from the trees. The sun's descent resonated the scene, causing ripples in the shadows between the rails. Here is where the discussion was to take place.

"I am in pursuit of the keys to liberation."

"Pandora's box is yet to be found ... but then again, the dunes have yet to reveal all their contents buried in the past."

"If anything, I'd require a digitized Pandora's box, more along the lines of an artificially intelligent entity."

"Assumption granted. Do you have any methodologies you are considering in the pursuit of such an item?"

"It will come to me. It always does."

"Faith and hope drag you deeper away from the truth."

"Light and truth are synonymous, for you, definitely not, for me. I much rather be in the darkness. There, I can truly be myself, alone, free of distraction."

"Maybe we are being too extreme. Consider the middle ground. The twilight."

"The transitional periods."

"Exactly."

"My calculations are indicative that these are the crucial times where experience converges with desire."

Alexey gazed at the horizon. Meyer tapped a beat to his leg, slow and calculated. They paused the conversation for a moment. A deep bellow.

The Attis Cult

The barriers to entry are insurmountable. Our investors would never go for it. Do you realize how much capital investment we would need to implement that type of strategy? We'd have to insure that investment, too, hedge aggressively and proactively in order to mitigate the risks of foreign currency appreciation. The Yen's been mysterious lately. I'd prefer to avoid that risk altogether. Unless, perhaps we could utilize derivatives and diversify our assets. The money markets. This is all pure speculation.

I had no idea what this guy was saying. I showed up at the tail end of a meeting, some A-grade conference room on the 25th floor of 53-story One Penn Plaza. Madison Square Garden's renovations could be viewed across the street through the mirror windows. The construction worker brawns looked so small in the face of the vast structure. We must have looked the same to them if they had been looking. I wondered if from their vantage point, was it like a giant Staples-sponsored dollhouse scene? It had been a long five minutes I had sat on the back couch when the determinant voice ached for my attention.

"Higgins, you get what I asked for?"

I nodded in assurance. He voiced his approval and levied me to approach the table, to sit amongst the corporation. They all sized me up, good thing I had worn a jacket even though it was the start of summer. Felt spry and capable with an Hermès tie left by my grandmother. The body next to me offered up a cigarette and I complied. I unveiled the contraband from my briefcase and shifted them to the center of the table. It was slick. The office tigers' eyes pounced and gleamed with zest. There was a silence.

"Sample. go right ahead." They complied voracious. I wasn't con-
cerned.

Vertex of a Boar's Tusk

The silence was normal. The darkness was more than usual. The bulb from the desk lamp in the adjacent room had blown out. The man did not feel like moving. He was sitting on a plush chair that had aged with lack of use. He continued to smoke. The shadows cut half his face in black.

The room had high ceilings, great stony walls adorned with woodwork. Out the window the moon shone across the rippling lake. Very few clouds but the occasional hoot from an owl in the woodlands. Afar on the opposing shore, where the tourists and passersby went, a great light cascaded to the purple sky. There had not been an explosion.

He put out the cigarette but remained seated, staring off into the water. The window frame sure made the cool night pretty. The distant light paved a yellow pathway across the dancing blue lake surface. Above the light were the mountain silhouettes reaching for the moon. This had been a most peaceful moment.

The man concentrated his gaze on the monitor. All the numbers were red. The investment had gone sour, and the partners had ran for cover. The digits red kept growing from right to left. He had already disconnected the landline and removed the battery from his mobile. He needed time.

The plans to take his allies to the beaches would have to be postponed. Instead, the old men would come calling with the pierced voices shrieking and clamoring for the sake of shareholder equity. Through this pack of smokes, he had developed a solution for escape.

This was a man of impeccable tastes and resolve. Separate suitcases lined his closet floor, fully packed and supplied for specific occasions. In this case, the least used one had to be utilized. This suitcase contained an MA-1 coat, black shirts, black cargo pants, and black combat boots. He wasn't going to the beach.

He went to the Land Rover Defender and drove through the forest to the radio tower. Here, he sent a message.

Then, he took the car and dumped it at a popular hiking site. Déjà vu, a bullrush flashback in the split atom of a second. Antiquity.

Exposition [1]

Somewhere along the southern tip of the bay in the fresh morning air, black smoke heaved to exorcism over the burning papers ablaze. Only the wake ups of the gulls and the serenade of shallow waves still swaying to the moon's growing distance accompanied the beat of crackling light before the sun could and would reveal its glorious might beyond the soft clouds and the blue sky with faded stars. Until the turgid whine of the sea jalopy came into range through the surface fog, only nature careened its course of shifting the contours of time and space.

The squib boat approached the tip where the blaze was finishing its purpose and then its operator could get on with his duties. From his mark below the stone walkway holding the fire, the only thought that reached the conception of words, even though he did not vocalize them, even under apathetic breaths and mumbles, was what a pile of garbage. Trash.

But at least this trash is going to proper waste, extinction, annihilation, eradicated through the flames. That at least thought, he did not say or put into words but revealed itself in a sigh to quit judging what had no claims to be judged. He noticed a lone publication ruining the water by the stern, the water still clear, and extended his right arm as he clung to the rail with his left and leaned his torso over the edge to get his two longest fingers to grip. After minute maneuvering, the publication clung to the hull stained with age and he hauled the collection of papers to a proper hold.

Avoiding the headlines and cover page proved inconsequential as he lost his footing for a moment, gathering the wet bundle from the dragging water. When the young man restored his balance and muffled a curse to himself for his sheer carelessness, the cover veered obliquely in his sight. The masthead marked The Spectator was jagged in a mutated fold on account of the dampness from the salt water and now had settled to a crusty milieu resemblant of a garment left too long to dry in a desert heatwave. Thereby, it only read Speator, the 'c' and 't' lost beneath the settled fold. The subtitles went bypassed as the young man casually inspected the cover art, at first curious, next baffled, and conclusively dismissive.

He had thought the old man on the cover, turned away from the reader, leaned over with one visible hand approaching an eye and the other hand crossed and gripped on a leg for balance, paid tribute to the thinker of antiquity, Rodin and all those that had submitted to his icon. And by the happenstance that a perception and concurrent thought shifts for a reason out of logical confines, he had considered, could it very be that the political puppet is soiling himself on the stones displayed, with no forgiveness, but rather gusto and empowering vigor. If only that sort of crude humor could be disseminated in jest without controversy, the old man's verdure could be organic filled with the amusement of a life well prodded as perturbative. The joke was not wasted as his mind wandered to await the event scheduled.

In these passings, he noted the stillness of the motion of the tide swaying gentle against the stone protrusion, the fog slipping beyond sight, and the disintegration of the fire's fuel through shades of grey smoke into cloud. Meanwhile, the coast where the driveway from the bay to the hard land was filling with darkened forms sticking out against the white-turned-beige homes and shops riddling the slopes into the lush foliage defining the outline of the village. Bellows of angst and crowded vistas gathered momentum and gravity upon occurrence, precipitous in waves as the snow gathers at a cliff prior to the avalanchian fall. And the young man remained on his arbitrary mobile land, the boat, separated by space and element, because he was not a participant in the cries for attention.

The buoy straddled along the current and a few seconds after the man's watch passed 06:30, the package revealed itself to the lighting air. He let it sit, peaking about between the buoy that cut it off from being a complete composition from the boat by the stony walkway jutting out to the crate of fiery papers and words and opinions.

It had been timed so the heavy ice could melt away and the light box could restore itself to the surface. Its contents were marked by the lack of care taken to their packing as the man harnessed the wooden container that held the contents onto his mobile land. This assignment was to be his last, he had determined, because he was plain sick of spending his morning in suspended motion.

It was not the boating or the waiting that bothered him. He could be on the sea forever and wait forever because that was normal, the passing of time. It was the uncertainty and the blame posed to him that had sickened his resolve.

For not three days ago, the man's supervisor had declared his deliveries to be unsavory and damaging reputations due to careless processing and handling. To which the young man had thought, in a much beleaguered cadence, how obvious did it have to be to be burdened and marked to him, alone. He was the handler, yes, but to what the packers and the processors and nature's course, how could blame be cast down to him, alone. Felt like folly. Hell, it had been folly. It was folly. He had kept these broodings quiet and let the snide man burnish his snide voice and his snide remarks to He, a silent recipient no more animated than a crumbling wall.

Still, now, on the waters of the summer lurking, his breaths felt sultry and even-paced. He had not considered a course of action to follow. He considered himself to be a man of his word and by default, he'd be sure to complete his duty, dispose of the package, and make a decision when the time for one was to be made.

The revolution was rotting to dust, skipped from a prospect of bloom and hope to spoil eviscerated. Of course, this dread applied to the young man and not the swarth congregated at the bay.

He envisioned women that had held his interest at the movement's start and two at the middle and none now that it was over for him. Snap shots of blurred faces cropped one in front on the other in his mind's eye. Then, regular mid-section outfits varied by breast size and ornamentation. Before he could go through the same process with the inverted V of the legs, the boom of gunpowder shook the fog and blue lights shone bright before fading into the upper fog.

It was almost seven and he thought he had best get back to the far shore of the island. The coast gathering would burn out as the barrel of papers had succumbed to ash.

Factorial Clockworks [2]

A former fishing boat depot converted to a center for conspiracy was always the destination. This time, the water was murky and smear black as the sun had lost its glare behind the fog blended with the cracked windows. The young man zoned out the sedating slogans inscribed on any wall space not reserved for press clippings and strategic frameworks. Since snide supervisor had stepped out, the young man turned up the phonograph from his mess of a desk. He did admit to sharing the snide's penchant for classical in the morning, though he'd never had said so.

The pamphlets' covers as brazen as any sort of propaganda made the young ma only feel contempt, so he flipped them on their backsides and he wished he had not kept his word. If he had not, he could have been at the grotto by then, with his camera and waited for the sun to come around again while he wrote in his journal. He folded some corners again just so they were consistent with the rest on account of the lack of care in the packing and the handling. With all the pamphlets laid out on the table, the young man placed the box by the other boxes to be used for other storings and a scrap of quality stationary stuck to one of the box's inner sides. All it said was Oggi, impulsively wrote like vandal text.

It could not be the cannon. That was no matter. He had always known as much as he felt safe to know, so what else could it be? Down the street and around the corner at the seniors' cafe, the papers would not say anything and neither would the old timers, for they were beyond affectation. No one knew how to let go better than an islander past the age of bronzed skin and fertile dreams.

There was dead silence poaching the streets. Not a live soul breaking the stillness and he met no one through the piazza on the way to his keep. Sure it was early but it was rather odd. The cannons on the mainland were muted by the distance and the neverending fugue of sea water wading back and forth. There was no destination to escape to. He'd still be seeking some thing and this was not a bother, only a truth. For his personal drama, he removed all the contents from his keep, left the key bent on the central portion of the beechwood desk, and departed with his knapsack and his few possessions.

Why had the ferry not come to port, he asked himself, as he set his body to motion, with the fate he'd eventually come to one meager thought he could claim clarity. He lapped the piazza and the port and the café and his former keep and still not a soul breaching his path to mirror his motion.

It made him feel relaxed. He fiddled with the matchbox on his pocket, half-filled, half holding mints, and rocked his lack of thought to the muffled clash of the objects stored. His pack did not feel heavy but he knew it'd become heavy to feeling if he lapped the path once more, and so, he broke the trodden path and traversed to the belvedere where not a soul came into sight or sound. Not even a street dog, or a cat, or a little gull, or a plane above. The cannons still sounded audible but in lesser waves of redundancy.

The way the soles of his shoes scraped the dirted earth and left traces along his carved path as the path laid its own gravel skin on said soles showed a route forward or backward, to and from, only destinations for brief breaks in the cycle. Gazing over the midday glass was respite from that revolution that was, at heart, an alien endeavor akin to the current. Sure there were great gains of momentum to be expected to culminate in crashes and aftershocks that could penetrate deeper shores, farther inland breached, but such an idealism summed in the term 'revolution' was a trend that would settle back to reflect-

ing the natural shadows and highlights before breezing to trivial in-
dulgence. He had known he was considered a lucky person. He had a
people. He had a cause. He had a role to play. Purpose came natural, as
long as he did not think about the grand scheme. This train of thought
was a greater damage than any wave the establishment could muster.

It burned his blood like an overcooked cotton left forsaken in the
sun to lose its colour and quality and result in a soft malleability. This
was not a thing to be valued, for him, but a thing to be shamed. And if
revolt was a bringer of a new establishment, what shame it had to de-
serve.

Intermission

That had all taken place in a far off country in a few years gone and it was good to not be so naïve. Any longer. The man was still young in looks and surface inclinations. It was his desires that had a nascent morphology. It had been American. Birthed of rebellion, bloody and controversial in execution, and gallant in greed, he was not a maximized revenue generator, but always, a capitalist. His position title was circumspect, for he had so very many specialized, specific roles to govern his duties as an agent for the customers' relations to the entity known as Mammoth.

Montage [3]

Mammoth had a centralized base in a megalopolis built on a swamp with excessive loads of concrete and buried wires, circuits, and vermin to inhabit the maze. Here was his source of freedom. His path to the Mammoth was, in essence, the same back and forth, but with the solid concrete and asphalt, it seemed only his soles bore the tread. The slabs could never cease. Only territorial pissings or excretions, bodily or painterly, may leave a mark. He, in most respects, got off on the anonymity to being an invisible comet. When he would burn out to a temporary station, this getting off reversed. For the omnipotent Mammoth was a chief purveyor of surveillance. Seek, survey, guide. A motto for the thought provoker. Provided resources, every thought could imbue knowledge onto a most entitled user, for reciprocation was tantamount to monetary success. What Mammoth lacked in physical product, it made up for with its subway frameworks. The executives preferred the tag "networks" but the young man, going henceforth, by the alias Mats Odon, thought there were no real nets and there was no real work to be done. It was 89 days to collapse, his freedom to be taken. Mats Odon defined this freedom makeshift, a catch-all for his ego. First, he'd marry. Second, he'd create a home. And, then, only then, could he finalize an absentee voter card. But, after the naïveté waned to null, and expenses created commitments, marriage, a home, and walled-off-by-distanceness were out of his spectral sight. The vanishing point that came into focus was one thing—escape.

Montage [4]

Idyllic whims, innocent paradises, just a purge from artifice and all its images. He had lost the capacity to think without imagining an image already manufactured and marketed to him for the sake of money. His self righteous pomp, he detested. Prescient contradiction toiled and he felt a nothingness, an absence, no content, no malcontent, something. If only there was still that grotto and that forest and an infinitesimal revolution, he could take his weekends in a private garden.

His daydream for freedom was not an obsession. It could never get to such a state because it engulfed all properties thinking at baseline.

On the 89th day, clocked out and back to the machine road home, he was not thinking. He had plans.

The plan was for eating and drinking and talking with a hypersexual woman. Mats had taken her to bed on many occasions and simply was not inclined to do so for any longer. He nixed the eating part of the plan so they could just meet for drinking and talking. It would be more lucid and cleansing. He always avoided the gluttony.

The woman, called Tara, was pretty on all fronts, insides, and backs. Lustrous hair, arched natural brows, bulbous green irises, eyelashes that needed no fakes, cheeks with constant bone contours, and lips the middle way that opened to a still-pretty jocular sweetness. She had been a dancer and her figure still showcased the nuances of such activity. She had not a clue how to dress proper but that was endearing to Mats because she could do casual and look classic.

But he would put her down nice and easy, 89 days ahead of time. Women, especially the ones possessing superficial vibrance, are thrown awry when a man denies their sexual advances. The sexual trump card has a tradition in the machine-oriented world to be played by the woman and the Woman, alone. Mats cancelled out the card. She was devastated. But could not see him as an evil mongrel of notoriously slanderous worthy rumor spreading and disrespect eternal.

All he had to do was change his eyes and the way he looked at her, to forget he had anything to prove. Mats smoked a cigarette and considered it a job well done to put a girl at ease without her hatred seeping unto him. He smoked and took in the pollutant air with tremendous guile for his accomplishment of such an impossible neutrality. But, then could it have been better to have been a vile terd and lie, so she could feel he was a lowdown, no good miscreant and she could conclude with a reaffirmation that she could do better. Now, he felt bad.

He smoked another. Was it selfish to be so nice and diplomatic about sex? They were not dating but he still felt he needed to eliminate the sex in an absolute finality. It was over with now, and he refused to let the cigarette tobacco be sacrificed any more tastes to the thoughts of imagining what goes on in the foreign corridors of the female cavity. He reentered the establishment and all visual cues had a transient vibe, that they were not quite there unless he would brush along their borders with a shoulder or a hip or a hand. The lighting looked less filtered. He had more liberty, less burden. And he thought she had, too. He was wrong.

*   *   *

Tara Thames was surfing on a metal board. She smiled to the foolish advertisements and kaleidoscopes of light-dark-light-dark through the blinks of stations and tunnel darknesses. That boy talked too much, about things, he got me thinking, thinking, thinking too much. What a sucker. He's a good kid. But I do need a replacement pitcher. He was a starter, but Hall of Fame, who could expect that now?

When she emerged from the subterranean, her mobile screen notified her of several free agents seeking her company. Her pressing responsibilities: to go home, water the plants, shower, and sleep to be at top notch form for tomorrow's mystery lost priority. She had to generally manage all the options in front of her, to begin a new transaction log. On her terms. Her omnipresent specter reverberating through the ceaseless rows of moving and stopping and standing windows and doors and lights and blank screens kicked her emotions. Empower that bravado. She was ready and she'd think later.

White powder, discordant synthesizers on oversized speakers, a button pusher, lots of lights raying out over the sweaty dance darkness. Latex, leather, baby powder. Deodorant, denim, poplin collar, grease. A symbolic exchange, filtered, an opening for two hours around the charge from late night to early morning, and back on feet. It seemed like no time.

Montage [5]

Mats Odon was back at Mammoth. He twirled a pen on his fingers because who had a need for a knife in this line of work. His hands only still had veins because he had done some real revolutionary work once, he kidded. It must have been the excursions on the ocean. Being so inland was a state of mind. The swamp city had water on all sides but not the right water.

Just calling it water was a travesty. The water connected, sure, grand scheme, but when Mats considered "waters," they were bodies, clusters individual and substrated to coalesce with their lone coordinates and relationships. He needed that kind of water.

Day 86. What kind? A river, a lake, an oceanblock. These were heavy considerations. The ocean was the grand ballroom, the arena, or a steady overture. But who needs a catch-all, especially if one has tendencies to gaze and daze and stay idle. No other body could compare, and he knew his preference could only be relative inland. The breaks were notable in parts of California but he had heard the Pacific was quite a dirty water. It could not be worse off than the Atlantic in the cold, but granted its size and the dry stark cold of the Western shores, perhaps it was. Lakes were pretty much negated by their borders so bare and he never liked boats, that is, boats on lakes. A river had the ceaseless linear trajectory and life's journey to look beyond, but he was not such a cabin guy.

His laziness did not lurk, it shone through and he decided on ocean. Ocean was the easy choice, free of conceptual considerations. No jellyfish. That was tantamount. But Mammoth executive 4 point 0 dash X.T. had orders.

*　　*　　*

Day 84.

Counter revolution had been the headlines. Elections were the demise of the revolutionaries transmogrified to bureaucrats and now, they were bearing the blunt of the force of the locking shackles of the media and mob tragicomedic machine. If they were smart, they'd make out okay with their investments and a consolidatory bill, before it was too late.

Mammoth executive orders had been fully delineated through the proper channels. This meant Mats Odon had a reason. He was to attend meetings in the field, paid to dress, eat, travel, shake hands, discuss, write, report, and underline figures to assure the executives that operations were performing, at the very least, equivalent to expectations. Variances were detestable and so, he did not pay much attention. See, he was checking on measurements previously observed and recorded and reported by an agent who had previously occupied his position and would be reviewed by a bilateral team of performance control committee members who would delineate calculation tasks to wage-slaving interns who would thereby report findings back to the team of committee members who would either choose to accept the results, sign them off, and return to conscious oblivion, or go back to the caboose and wait for the whole diseased enterprise to make its way back to their bottlenecks at an indeterminate time before quarterly statements were to be due.

Mammoth was not a bad place. The corporate structure accommodated its members, Mats included, with amenities akin to a hotel, only the amenities were worldwide and pervasive to penetrate any connected cosmopolitan transway. If there were electrical impulses and artificial projectors, you could be sure that you could get a perk, even for a can of tuna or a roll of toilet paper.

Mats was particularly fond of the steam room at the locker chamber and the wave breaker. Water, mankind, water. The message was quite convincing. Do the assignment, keep any thoughts of disorder tight shut, and the salary and goods could keep being stacked and acquired. A healthy system.

He felt dumber by the hour. His boss served as a school boy seer, with the contingent cynicism and dead stare but his witticisms had long ceased to rake up any dissent or amusement on Mats' part. Was he a drone, and was he not bothered by the sentiment?

After lunch, his desk was free of clutter, so he placed a few stacks of one-year-old documents beside his writing hand. Then, a screen bound in leather with a Gary Cooper movie accompanied by subtitles and a notepad the same size in case he need cover it. He hadn't the need so far.

Ten minutes went by and the heels of thunder knocked the tile forty-five degrees portside. Heels of Thunder was a figurine dedicated to oodling, drooling, flapping, and hair tying and waving. She did a nasty surface service. Intentions were discounted for the effects of sedation her strut could augment.

See, the male underlings had been the chief culprits of the grandest scheme Wooly had ever executed. Wooly, Mammoth's parent company, had launched a peer-to-peer, user-friendly, database search substrate of viewing pleasures, provided advertisements to their affiliates (owned and operated by Wooly's subsidiaries and partners) were permanently bordering the links to the pleasurable viewings. They were specific and nonjudgmental and the underlings had grown accustomed to having their hands' hyperspeed ejaculation, because, they had to be honest, it was efficiency at its most core display.

Thereby, Mammoth had a living, breathing, cumbing organism made up of multidimensional cells very rarely multiplying who could be set at ease for six to twelve hours a day by worthy, capable shunner who enjoyed synoptic responsibilities. Hooking was so obsolete.

Montage [6]

Streaming, innovating, building the feature future, one purged excretion at a time. Mats thought the death of sex drive could be a good thing. At the cost of freedom, he could make due and pursue his ego cultivation. But as day 84 came to a clock expiring close, he began to fear the fire embers starting their smoke in his bloodstream. He would have need of a companion in his freedom but his sacrifice kept him masked from the folly of his worry. What could Tara Thames be doing? Looking good, knowing she looked good, and doing something that required looking good, because that is what she was meant to do. It always looked better looking good while doing anything.

Mats lit a smoke. No, no, it could not be so absolute. She was a fine thinker, but it made it easier to justify his lack of courtship and sportsmanship in the pursuit of the feline. She was so easy to catch that it just spoiled. But he still wondered what a creature, like herself, free to roam and operate on those God given legs, could be doing. Maybe it was a distraction from the itch behind his slacks hugging his ass.

Tara Thames was at yoga. She was not wondering about Mats Odon. She was not wondering at all. That was not important. But the way she controlled her breath and meditated on her volition to wield her body were privy endeavors.

Then, she was at a luncheon with an ad woman she knew from college. Ad woman wanted to show off and Tara did not mind.

"I came three times last night," ad woman declared with bravado. It had been fun. Tara Thames nudged her chin down and gave an open smile. Women don't grin. Ever. They smile. And Tara smiled, her teeth shining on ad woman.

"When's the last time you came, babe?"

"I don't want to talk about it."

"Babe, babe, now, don't be like that."

"I got dumped but we weren't even dating."

"The 21st century, babe, let's get you back on the field."

"Please. It's just, I'm having withdrawals."

Ad woman's face lost it. She had heard rumors but Tara's confession was the first prime speaker she had encountered. Could it be, the tables were turning, the grand cocksmen were endangered and upon breach of the holy cavity, addiction was incurable. Had she, actually stumbled out of a true diamond drill?

Tara saw ad woman's eyes and immediately regretted the tongue slip. Putting the stance out in the open, the word of mouth, had notorious consequences. Abstractions became tangible. Recording phonetics were secondary to the omnipotent network and its prime instrument, the camera. For with expert or amateur accounts and computer-driven statistical mining, data could be extracted and the sounds could be mimicked to an approaching asymptote in accuracy. Absolute meant 90, 95, or 99.7 percent confidence intervals and margins of error were mere signposts for legal protection. Disclaiming reality.

Heck, Tara knew that the split second impulse and exercise of that impulse, to declare an event, had made it real to some one and thereby some thing greater than her or this wildebeest of a cavity opposite her at the table. Wars could be waged on the open market.

"This is a breakthrough, Tara. Oh my gosh, do you realize how ground breaking you really are? We cannot even joke about it unless more frontierswomen have the courage you so possess."

"Is that not an overreaction? You cannot be serious."

"I am lively in my seriousness. No dead serious. Live serious. Hear me out. Fancy me. I feel as if we're closer, closer now than ever before. Let's do some shots."

"Look. It's kind of embarrassing. I do not, under any circumstances, want this coming back to me. I know what you do for a living. No eyewitness claims. No nothing." And Tara could already see the nefarious conception of the ad campaigns for the verminous products capable of mongering the market in to a new gender conscious render.

The shots were already here on the table. And like a marble losing its luster in softening light, the details faded and the dancer in the darkness between her thighs needed a fix.

Montage [7]

The pool water had a foreboding glare. There were bronzed legs leaving trails of rot and flesh and oily, oily excrement via perspiration striking concrete and chlorine-infiltrated water. A cesspool as the lovers of every modified simple moral quandary. These people claimed they were not thinking. Yet, she, in the white tube top, across the pool by the edge of the sky river, stroked her hair and sucked in her diaphragm to augment those glorious coconuts protecting her pump engine, was deep in a tunnel, the bullet train of thought blocked by so much intersecting, logjamming traffic. She had heard and she now wondered in plain sight.

Was one of these strappers a qualified harbinger for her release point? Was the man with bluer eyes than the glow of the water of the pool capable of timing, reading the motions of the flux, and catching on, and standing to declare balance and reach a watermark that could be his own in her own torrential downpour tube? Or was it the hefty bearded man boy in an Octopussy tee shirt and vomit-flavoured jeans that could raise a tree and clear out her gridlock? Or was it the colt-like rocker that was too pretty for drugs, any longer, that could give her a perfect cruise and drive and ride and then simmer into a content rest bar?

Which one possessed the holy tool? The mystery abounded and she thanked the cosmos her cycle had coincided in its conclusion with the pseudoevent shaping before the peripheries. She was not stroking her hair or fixing her person with her limbs, just the breathing and the mind. She looked smooth doing it.

Some oaf nudged her arm in a passing to take a route to the bar and he smiled nonjudgmental as he did it to negate the interruption and then he passed her on. A trivial dismissal but to her, a sign of a dark note, so perhaps the beat could kick back and rise into a cerulean spell of fancy. She saw her girlfriends across the pool fiend for well-decorated cock, grotesque with their showcases of wealth. Not one, not two, but three gold chains. Sheer shoes that looked like latex beyond a twenty foot range. And straw fedoras that polarize impulses to either slap to the gutter or to consider, hey, I should get myself one of those, they'd complement my features and go with my boat shoes. Brah.

The handsome brutes in raw denim and tasteless glory exuded bestial confidence and the dance to the dungeons was playing out in steady beats. Wide chins widening with smirks and snickers and slams of fists and strikes of male bondage. Was it not so much fun that she should get in on the action?

The bald bard Henri latched a stable hand onto her mid-back and whispered, "what's wrong, love?" She looked at his eyes through his coke-bottle glass lenses and there was care there. The gays were wild. Sure, she still felt his libido yet he'd never exercise it. It was these particular crowd members, instead of going for the pants, their self-professed limit was the surface and perhaps a necking session to conquer adolescent missed and rejected results. She felt bad for this springboard morbidity and condescending digression.

"Nothing's wrong, babe."

"Let me get you a drink." And scurried off before she could politely decline. At the very least the music was not so loud up here, on the roof. The open air gave the feeling freedom still governed the space. She was stupid.

"Hey, I'm Guy. What's your name?"

She looked at him, then hesitated, then said, "Tori."

"Tori, that's a hot name."

"Oh, thanks, Guy."

"So, like you want to go dance, these beats are sick, right."

"No. Thank you."

"We got bottle service in the VIP section downstairs. Just say. my name and we got you." And he started walking away. And he stopped short and capped. "Look, you were all alone and it's just a friendly invitation. You have your date or your girlfriends or it's just you, you're welcome. And then, you actually do, and you have fun, and you talk to me or my friend, and maybe you decide this person isn't a total scumbag, but, hey, what do I give a fuck?"

Strong-armed, she was almost impressed. Her shit-kicking bodyguards approached with Henri and shots galore. The confluence of pure spectacle overloaded her senses with sabotage. She had no free will. Only standing and silence. Because she would not dare leave, storming off to peace. No, no, she could never. Because she'd offend her girlfriends and that was a pure detriment to even the coldest of felines.

She knew she was stupid. She had come here. She had to come here, she believed. And now that the decadence fed her, she was stuck here. It was an expected baseline of recurring idiocy and seminal amusement. And the point was, she was wearing a tube top, she should just wait and some schlub would serve her fine for a session, however deep down the depravity circuit she'd like to go. Her bodyguard dudes encouraged the shots and cheered Karoomba. They went and took the girlfriends across the pool and declared spoils, lifting them over shoulders, kicking and singing siren calls, away from the straw-hat-helmeted assclowns, and plopped Tess and Tasha beside her.

"Be real friends," bellowed from bodyguard Berenger and his role was done with karma. Bodyguard Boyle plus Berenger absorbed the darkness and disappeared into the swarm, seeking.

"Liz, let's go, come on now."

She didn't respond, maybe because she had so gotten used to going by Tori that night. She realized. "Come on where?"

"Candy says, candy goes."

Perfect icebreaker. Lines, purposes, roles, cards, bills, and sensuous pleasures. Definitions. The mirror was always extra friendly after intake.

Liz was here, the moment was hers. She looked like she wanted a quick fix and she should suck it up and quit her thought.

The three took to Guy's table and the bodyguards were busy necking inexperienceds on the masquerade cattle drive coaxed in flashing lights and spilling souls.

An hour or so later, she had Guy's guy get the manager and get him to the side where she did not have to yell. She needed a car home, she was feeling sick. Guy's guy paid for it and she sucked back into the vacuum of empty streets and empty faces. The window filter was a saving comfort.

She kept thinking she should have done more, done more, been fed more, talked less. Whenever the lines latched her orifices, she shifted roles and became an active player.

This was bad. She considered it superior in form and class and times to be passive, a filter, an observer of the spectacle. To play witness to the farcical drama always was more dignifying. The man's stage was the table and they deserved what they had paid for. Prettiness, friendliness, fakeness probably, and maybe a party favor in the form of a tug, a rub, a sucky suck, or if they really were patient, room serviced release.

The guy at her right knee, the one she kept bumping into by accident, had flummoxed her coke kick. He was not friendly. He was not high. And he was not interested. He had to be but he did not show it. Lots of did nots, lots of wonder.

They smiled at each other once and he looked away, sunken into his seat and chugged all his drinks in petty silence. Guy and Tom and Bob tickled him once and nudged him abhorrently yet he remained transfixed on being a lone in the group. He was too good looking to have a shitty significant other lurking amidst the stained carcass of the once industrious complex. Heck, maybe he was a priest.

The car was notably clean and notably independent. As if it'd been in a personal garage. The smell, the absence of dust, the way the leather still had pep, so she asked the driver if he knew who was paying for the car.

"Personally? In rhetoric?"

"Yes, I want to thank whoever did this for me."

The driver hesitated, almost chuckled. The light was red. "Honey, are you playing me?"

"Excuse me."

"My apologies ahead of time, but the rule goes, anyone met at a club is a one time thing."

"I'm no slut." She got out of the car and walked strident. The driver lumbered the German landboat up to her side.

"Miss, please. It's just a rule. I'm not giving any judgments. I'm just the driver."

Liz continued silence and stride.

"It's my job to get you home safe, regardless of the context or the offense taken. Get in the car."

"How dare you? I can get the police."

"Please, honey. Be reasonable, responsible, have a heart." The crosswalk showed STOP and she could not pass through on account of the droves of people deliveries in peak hours.

She got in.

Montage [8]

The Journal the Monday first in the new fiscal quarter unveiled a leaked coup to be staged to extricate a bunch of assistants, secretaries, deliverymen, mailmen, custodians, and marketing teams to a newly formed partnership entitled Casbah Snows.

The news did not bother Mats, he was almost up to expiration date, day 74, specific, and here and behold, he had a reason to poach at Tara, not for sex, but for a more abstract sort of spoil.

Charity.

See, Tara made him feel evil inside bent up like roadkill infested by the life cycle, like he was instigating a plethora of negative energy abounded and situated all on her jocular, beautiful self. And this impending force of pendulum karma could undoubtably swing back and kick him in the balls. He feared this sort of evening out.

Should he have sex out of charity? No. But he could show a true platonic inclination and act on it by securing her a position in the case of her layoff doom. Hereby guaranteed by the report the Journal advertised. She was an ad hoc data analyst, efficiency manager with capable tools of flexibility and resource allocation and distribution, specifically in the cosmetic corporation sphere of affairs.

Her agency fielded job offers from Mammoth and Wooly and all the rest, so he could catalyze her with a security blanket position as a lasting parting gift. And she'd never have to know it was via his agency. It was not a duty but an obligation and the karma virtue could be insured.

It was a shitty idea but he thought his active love had a ripple effect of positive whims.

Mats stopped his conscience from overcooking the recipe. It's never a good thing to think oneself into paralysis, he always reminded himself. His inner voice spoke in a grave monologue, slow and profound in frowning upon reprobations. The voice never had a fully visible face, just a gaunt, extra-wide chin, slithering lips, and shadows starking the jaw into the black hood. A monk on a vibrant purple and red and crimson yellow gorge tainted by the valley's decay and blight of the gravitas. For in serious matters, and this was a most morally incongruent matter, hence, serious, the voice of the bard biblical summoned his mind to answer, to be compliant, and if not, be cast out in shame and folly to find his way back to the repentant, repugnant road.

Defeat was better left avoided. He decided to gamble on the State versus State track meet because it was individual and felt excretory, an exorcism of some bent up, self-conjured angst.

The results were to be received by the time he was to end his drone dealings. And if he won, he would have an excuse to be in a good for nothing spirit.

Montage [9]

The personal drama took manic highs and lows with too much cerebral dosage. No one is that important, least of all, You. So, Mats reiterated, underscored, lapsed into drone-dum. Walking home anonymous one day, you forget, he noticed a billboard flashing individualized and signatured opinions about daily cultural foci. He saw a name way too damn familiar and the quote, "a real revolutionary fights from the inside."

He threw up a little in his mouth, gagged, coughed, lit fired tobacco. So, that's the end result, where it had come and burned out. The revolution got sucked into the political circus, they got their publicity, and now, they had legal sponsorships. Selling out did not bother him. It was the lack of privacy, the individual thoughts were not so individual. They were just renderings of the same thoughts spun black, white, zig zag, faux pas, and they could not be stopped. Gradients. Granularity. Conformity.

It had to be personal though. Otherwise, he probably could have avoided the stomach churn consequence. The flash flood images of water aided his passing dissent and some mysterious legs of a feline. They stood still in the water, like cranes with a pulse, the water massaging, transforming, adapting to the presence. Who could she be? Definitely not Tara Thames.

He had a voicemail. It had been Thames. He decided to wait.

Montage [10]

Three days and three more messages. Each, monotonous, no revelation of discomfort, insecurity, or urgency. She did say, "it's important." It could not have been that important if she did not raise any voice cues and so he ignored it.

She did not call for a while. He had an IT guy, that owed him for a daily double tip he refused to forget about, initiate Thames into the pool of accepted applicants. He was done. He could escape via karma and it felt so good to be so selfish.

The megalopolis swamp weather was in the stretch of consistency prior to the looming winter snow purge. Scattered pockets of rain rebooted the wayward sunflowers picketing their life forces on irresponsive promenades and avenues. The miserable trees leaned down if they could not catch enough sun and dragged slow and slow to grinding collective squallidry. The trees that could get lucky enough to reach sun were vastly taller and stronger and more engaged in ignoring the pauperous affairs below. Was it the sun that got them that way or the haphazard fate that belies the position at start?

Thames dreamed of flight. To get away from it all. She had this tidy job offer presented to her lap with a virtual ribbon and guaranteed monetary allure. It was a sign of the city devil. Just as she longed to leave, she felt pulled right back into the engine works. Ad woman called her and she did not pick up and she inquired why Odon had not responded to her calls.

The irony was ghastly. Here, alone, unfettered, not in the throngs of copious defiling, Tara had an opportunity to make Mats the wealth he needed to get away.

If he would only be privy to her initiative, then he could be lit to the flight that she so desired.

Her hands felt dry. Her nails looked like plastic. Were there wrinkles and death marks gathering beneath the knuckles, she should wear gloves everywhere during the day, she thought, good for the aging process.

Tara sought to spell it out so simple, and plain, to Mats. It was not even about his dick, though, of course, the entire opportunity was dependent on his willingness to make a mindful decision beneficial to his dick.

Oh the folds in the strips of the paper waving through the gusts of machine driven winds through the nihilistic streets were being grounded by the ballistic might of gathering raindrops and all Tara could wish was for a pleasant spa. She dialed Mats' number but hung up before connection reached. She called ad woman. Strategy needed shifting.

Montage [11]

Mats Odon was steaming, meditating, stretching, sweating, escaping, resetting.

His moment was compromised. In the form of heavy breaths, dragging feet clapped with plastic sandals, and an endearing belly well fed by steaks and sins. His boss of his boss of his team of bosses made an appearance, his head garbed in a towel like a turban, hiding the lack of hair, or rather, eschewing the sweat glands to concentrate on the supreme brain.

Damascus Dieter was a billionaire. He was a legitimate iconoclast, as far as that term could reach a limited liability partnership and an interfaced estuary of Delaware, Cayman Islands, and Swiss incorporated charters.

The steam barricaded eye contact. Once Dieter coordinated his heartbeat to the gong of the steam, he sought conversation. He revealed with a head bow.

"Pleasant day, Mr. Dieter?"

"Pleasant company, Mr. Odon."

"How did you know it was me in such a place?"

"I could ask you the same thing."

"I suppose, presence is beyond."

"Let's leave it at that."

Dieter had the floor.

"Water?"

"Surely."

Dieter raised his sails and embattled through the smoky transience until he silhouetted through the translucent door into black and vanish. The cooler sounded like a toilet flushing in slow motion and Mats closed his eyes until Dieter returned bearing life's elixir in oversized plastic cups overflowing with spillage. Absorption. Camaraderie. Intrigue.

The men drank. Dieter began, "what do you feel about leaving the company?"

"Uncertainty, all its merits and pains."

A pause.

"So, there are no defined plans?"

"Travel."

"You seem to still be developing these arrangements."

"I am more curious to know how you seem to be so personal."

"Comes with the job. Universal human conditioning."

"How's it go? A man's concerns ..."

"... are any man's concerns."

"Run for office, sir."

"Boy, you do not run for office. You dance behind closed doors in another man's office."

"Your enemy's office?"

"If only you could decipher your allies from your foes."

"Come out with it plain, sir. I've been cooking for too long."

"Out of decency, ye shall be rewarded. Can you guess?"

"A bonus or an extended array of perks."

"Come to my office."

"I thought I was already in it."

"The door's open."

It was odd. The steam room door was open, as if on a timed lever. The steam cleared out. Mats rose and left. He closed the door, Dieter brooding in the darkness, as a rottweiler chews his raw meat. The steam clacked on and valves fired.

Thank God for the shower, was all Mats could think. As he concluded, the steam door remained close, the valves humming, and the red light insinuating onward to transcendent possibility. Once he stepped off the Mammoth grounds, he began to think. He stopped. This subterfuge required misjudgments, so he headed to the bar.

Montage [12]

Day 66.

A rebel from the past. The arson expert, who drummed along with the smack of the tramps of the boots against plazas. He also had a mohawk. He spit black. His teeth were fake and yellow, nonetheless. No beard now, this had shocked Mats.

Phillip Burlik had tracked Mats' movements and upon deciphering Mats' bi-weekly sojourn to binge at the local pub, he had made contact. In a place devoid of lucid minds, he felt safe. His hair had grown to cover the ink tattoos of extreme zealous convictions, a great telephoto lens on the back of his head and waves tidal on both sides, all covered by curly black bard hair.

"It grew mighty fast."

"That's the way you greet a loyal dissenter."

"I see you. You need money?"

"No. How dare you?"

"How dare I what?"

"You need to meet a friend."

Montage [13]

The way it played out, internal control was to have the last laugh. That was how Mats considered all viable outcomes, be it as there were plausible determinations compressed and catapulted into nascent orbit to smash and smite upon agents' appropriate roles. Encroachment struck deep seeds to fester into malignant growths, in which case, an always natural backlash could reset the established quo. It was such a sense of foreboding on day 66, red black clouds acidic in mushy solidity, almost like scabs on a desert horizon, then was the rain and the concurrent slime that desalinated skins, garments, and stones. Maybe there were signs of tread, just man was exiled from nature's elementary potency.

The meeting with the boss had been confirmed via a necessary messenger personally directed to his kill-time compartment. Just the concept and realization it was an actual live bodied meat-eating, phone-screen junkie reporting this information face-to-face, heightened the suspenseful possibilities of an old time in an older country.

It had not been so far gone. He still had the smells and if they were faint on a humid day where the fumes were too strong to prevent any thought but irritation for the present, Mats Odon had an idea of the feeling conveyed and truly conceived to his core. This certainty was critical in such a sterile environment. He blocked out all the realities of the disgust accumulated over the course of the business cycle. He blocked them out.

There were doors and elevators and then there could be portals of transmutation. This was such a mixture, for the doors vanished beneath, no walls auxiliary, and upon entry, it was an elevator horizontal, more a monorailed standing room, and the sights showcased were the cityscapes above 675 feet, maybe higher. Here, the clouds had pockets, colors natural to a grayed, musk city eschewed in blightful malady and mayhem. Here, it was a change in perspective, a tilt on the gameboard, or becoming In on the joke one has been the bane of and just had not realized its ubiquity.

No automated projections appeared. It was Mats in the spatial void and he'd have time to gather thoughts and brood over how the past had come to matter so strongly at the bearings of his mind's compass. On day 66, better yet for antiquated taboos, Mats considered, not antiquated enough to extinction. Now, good man, focus on the task at hand. Temptation, Incentive Packages, Signing Bonuses, Stock Options. ALL poison. You've had the money. So why do you not run?

Set-ups negated victory or loss. It was a matter of chance's hand and its sleights in risky variability. All outcomes were predetermined and prepared for in accordance with algorithmic statistical substructural support. Correlation does not mean causation—what a pile of horse crud.

Could one smoke in the portal? He'd wait until he arrived at the destination. The portal continued on a horizontal path when it shifted to a constant sloping trajectory upward at a snail's rate across an asphalt road. Perhaps there had been vomit cases. There had to be another, more sensible gateway. This fuss had to be a stunt, or maybe it was the luxury of passing time in a harmonious state, instead of rubbing elbows with sweat-stained heat hens and wrinkled, 3-day worn sock shots poaching the conditioned air. Elevators. His nature had overridden all sentiments of arduous tranquility and mirthful gaiety, for the Mammoth Enterprise just threw too much in his face for it Not to. For that was the point. And here is where the story takes a turn back to the far off time, when revolution was a reality, not a commodity.

Interchange

The horizon showed nothing but a fog-casted hue of torment and doomed dares. Bespeckled lurked the muddled shops of craftsmen long bankrupt and billowed away in mass throngs to forsake the places they had filled with organic love. These were to be the perfect safehouses.

Now, before this became apparent to the passenger, the driver bombasted an egregious account of the weather and the destination. The passenger, thought to himself, it could be much simpler if the driver had focused on the winding road ahead and the entry to the woodlands, so as he could see the surprise at the destination come the proper time and movement. Effortless to zone out, for the sight of the tiny blotches of ink on the horizon, the apparent safehouses to be, were beyond proximity to convey a magnanimous impact. Closer were the rolling hills adorned with sheaths of prairie material and light winds swaying the sheaths like a celestial harpsichord player. A soothsayer's melody, enchanted by the clear cast sun too high that it looked the sky was a ceiling, and the shadows were smooth accents on a golden gradient of autumn foliage nectar and new before the fall of the winter.

Here, the passenger had a slow and steady beating heart, distracted from the task to be, if only were it not for the amoral oaf straining the driveshaft, could this journey truly be a meditation. It would have to suffice in his mind alone, and alone ahead on the road, the avenue of acacia trees lined the light like keys on a piano over the cool asphalt at the final leg of the straight.

At the fork, at least the driver retreated to his inner voice and the shared sounds of engine and wind through the angled mirror windows blended in harmony with the steady drull of a Louisianian jazz oracle and the wail of a mournful guitar.

Reinvention, renewal, washing away the trodden path and into the maze of the woodlands, ideas began to fester. For the future was on verge to be held the instant they were to find the road out of the wooded maze. The pleasure of roads was the ease at which destinations could be divulged. Directions showed for directions' sake. Natural purpose and function. Chaos was a foreign concept.

The passenger jostled his hand, tap, tap, tick, on his worn denim leg to the sorrowful psalm, crying, "where did she sleep last night ... my girl ... my girl don't ..."

It was pleasant to have been in the company of men, at the operational control center, at the mission briefing, at the printing press, at the docks, at the garage, at the shoreline, and after the assassination. No distractions, sure, yet in the fastidious flurry of activity, sweeping the future into a merry-go-round of presence, the passenger assuaged limber longings for a woman as the endgame. Whoever the concept could possess and channel through a flesh and blood state was the boon when these obligations were fulfilled, when orders were carried out, and when a rebus for fortune and content was to be a bassline for daily life.

Immediate sights interrupted the dream daze, and as the driver smashed the volume knob off, the focal point was the bloody man in the road, arms high and wielding for help, and the car mangled in chaotic shambles around a defiled acacia.

The passenger stayed in the car, and loaded the two-shot that had been tucked beneath the seat. The driver had left, approached with caution and kept a fair distance from the man disguised in distress. He was reciting a rehearsed context, it had to be. The passenger noticed the driver's motions ossify into caution, his hand veins more pronounced, his legs straighter, his feet cemented into striking pose. It had to be a plant. The man did not have a mark on his hands. This was ambush.

The Bearclaw was ready.

A struggle ensued. A cutter's knife came out. The knife beamed in the high light, the driver looked like a soldier transfixed in a tug of war, conjuring all his volition to lift the flag to stand, to prevent the knife from serving its master's desires.

The passenger stepped to the open. The distressed man fell back, the driver had swept the leg. The, the Bearclaw fired. Heaves, huffs, gravity. The driver lay stomach side dead and bloody, crisping against shade-free asphalt.

The passenger shunned the distressed man and let him rise on his own accord and pick up his chosen weapon. The distressed man had no longer to be distressed and was just a man now, a survivor, and strode shoulder width apart the passenger, both staring at the wreck of the American roadster and the mess of a fresh spoiling body.

"You had to use the Ford."

No response.

"It just had to be the Ford." The passenger stressed each word, and peered at shoulder side.

"Lad, it was the only available."

"Blast!"

"Let's get on the move. Our contact is rather fidgety."

"He can wait. The Ford is my concern."

"It's a sunk cost. There's no salvage value in a broken machine."

"Sentimental value is a fallacy, but one I declare mine. Let me see her once more."

"The drama of this ego. You fool, you're driving."

"Phillip." The man waited to get in the car.

"What, Mats?"

"You got any fuel?"

"Always for a steady subvert." He unveiled a leather bound flask and it glid through to Mats' bind. Mats tossed back the coach gun and Phillip caught it like nothing.

"Guard that cargo. I'll drive."

WIPE

[1 4]

The door was unlocked and the merciless hallway forced Mats to comply. The memory had no afforded time left. Business meant presence. Mats knew he was to be on capable guard. Dieter had renowned skill in subterfuge and the steam room had just been a reconnaissance run, not even a warm-up. Mats was already in his territory. At heart, the only danger was to be convinced he'd want to remain.

Dieter stared at the horizon above the clouds and through the gateway framed by the twin peaks of radio towers twenty blocks downtown. He looked down on them. We were on higher floors, the vantage point of despotic sorcery, and Mats could admit it was a position of privilege, just being up here, astray from the public. No delusions of grandeur in such an environment. Only plausible possibilities that required planning and execution. No real need for imagination. Just look at the room, look at the windows because of this room. Strategy was sourced in such rooms.

Here he was. He did not take a seat. He entered Dieter's frame and lit a cigarette.

Dieter stayed seated, gauzed in authority, like a boulder on a hill, immovable to the battles struggled below. Odon eventually sat, too, and what was exchanged was an excavatory quality between their eyes. For, there was some unspoken idea that was just the crux of the context, and after more cigarettes and a firm agreement, Mats shook Dieter's hand. Dieter stood up and Mats was to have a signing bonus and extra income, without extending his stay. Day 66 had all the makings of fortune striking and lushing out Future.

Mats too kindly to going off the grid. The grid was the semi-public permeable forum for which he had had the utmost privileges to engage with the khaki warriors and leg-heel-leg combos such as Thunder Heels and all her granularities, et cet era et cet era. But now, he was moving on up in appearances and realities, no matter how he cut the cake or the corporate claims for equal clamor.

Physically, closer to the top, more westward, actually, no, more northeastern, these coordinates were confusing with the interchanging zig zag of the ziggurat building hallways. And the greatest affectation was that when the rare instance, another human form came by in the corridor, he-she immediately bows his-her head down in reverence or precursory apology, because if Mats were staring up to the distance, he de facto encumbered authority and he so desired his privacy. Like a star actor, making eye contact to get kicked off set. Not all stars were such squaws and Mats certainly considered himself a vulture but one that was not in need of a muzzle or a sedative. Still, he had a semblance of authority and he embraced it, isolatory.

His office was quite spectacular in gaudy ornamentation. As if it was a museum piece, like those coloured rooms on the White House tour. Equipped with the LED lit computer machine screen interaction and a few cords camouflaged into the azure carpet, one could have guessed it was clearly after the Baroque period but still the designer must have had an affinity for Victorian pomp plus dainty dainty daint. Buffalo.

A great carcass must have once been attached to the head. Was this legal? No matter, Mats sat in his arm chair, the kind.

Mats Odon's nights went by on a smooth metronome pulsating to the sleeping beats of the forgetful Night. Never had such ignorance been so innocuously blessed in the guise of self-capsulate mirth, for what work there was to be done, could be done tomorrow. What myriad example of designer activities, the industry, it'd be all for nil for there was no tomorrow, in a pencil pusher's rat in a cage agenda suicide. But he, no, sought space, and ye shall be granted the kingdom of corporation once you sell your soul a little. The revolutionaries all did it, only they needed better role models.

The quintessential embodiment of the marketing media parade—the quarterback. The great Dane of Men, the K-9 pack lead of the gladiator kin, wielding the chaos for a split second spiral through the V, obtuse, acute, sometimes beyond shape, between Riddell helmets, concussed heads, juiced respirations, wont on struggle, the holy circus. Spectacular pom poms and the romp of the mob's collective bloodlust shirking all congregation for peace and tranquility. Ye the quarterback could right the comet of the motions emotional of the crowd and seeking glory, upon possession, so was the crowd appeased and sated. With such a constant wave of euphoria of the plebeian hearts and corporate bottom lines riding on the gunslinger. No deaths, just cuts and waivers and agency. Franchise tags, the greatest coup of all time. Your short term, my bottom line, I win. See, they'd all been accustomed to it. The price of success. So, now, in the twilight of the participatory years, embrace the political spa, it's where all the true dollars pass hands, it's self-declared arbitrage, switching commodities, you may as well be gambling at the place you own and operate.

Watch the next car commercial by the retired Super Bowl quarterback. You can learn a thing or two. Stay straight narrow arrow and ye shall be sated. Just expect consistency and kitsch cuckolding, suffocation of the soul. Spirituals, such pussies.

Now, Mats had a new print on his wall, for the sake of irony and for the notion he was an utmost joker for his precarious situation. What had he but the dream enlivened, he did not even have to go to work to complete work. In such an objective separation from his previous post, in the trenches of cubicle-Clorox drone-dom, he could have a heart because they were on the same team. Now, he was not required for such a sacrifice. Yet, what he would give to observe and not even report, but just take in his eyes and ears and the smells and the motion and the moments between where the entire world seems to be sedated in free fall, that you've been falling down the precipice into the abyss for an eternity that you've given up on any suspense or expectation. May as well be walking around with C4 taped to your chest or just realize the drones are the fulfillment of the nuclear warhead threat. They're war toothpicks. Still death inductive geysers of foreboding doom.

In the privacy, he missed watching the market fizzle and swell back and forth and the slants and sins and tangents and trigonometric arrangements between the sexual mores, the trinity, the sluts, the two shoes, the way faces change under the fluorescent light because the sunlight is so numbing in the pallor of bullet-proof, suicide-proof glass that you are in an observation tank and there are infinite aquariums bursting all around so the only reality you can observe is the other side of the same coin. He even had it framed, beechwood stained black with minimal flare. George Bellows, the Fighters, the Struggle, the Image. See enough of something and it swallows you and spits you back out, because no matter how much you may seek to deny the spooky serendipitous swirl of objective reality, the axiomatic basis for the quantum quarks and barometers of measurement and concurrent definitions, you know there exists no concept that can be cosmically explained through the preordained inevitable that words and speech and the way you butterfly effect everything from the spout beam spewing and telling you to do this and that because the weather is a certain way and your jeans feel a certain tugness and your back feels taut and your hands like they are the life force and when you are able to just visualize and see with the eyes that you can displace the body bag membraning your bubble and just project into the image, the diaspora of organisms into surreal Oz, sober dosed. Classical music helps, or the end of the heartache.

He forgot what it had been called. He had to look it up. Maybe he'd take up oils again, he finally had a reasonable income that did not feel like stealing. It was exactly the way it should be. Best to block out the morality, only for the self-professed victims. My tough luck, he thought, I'm beginning to sound like a fascist. Well, the tag is a relative because tomorrow, the fascists may be the heroes. What a twisted thought.

He turned on the sports channel. Time for further fantastical phantasmagoria. The daily beagle. Brawn Bellows. What came with the boxing. The leather against perspired adversity, skin on muscle on piping. And the cackle of harlots, and the smoking of time, and the gorge of the crowded Cerberus, letting the gates stay open for a brief flicker in the glow of the candle of the dead and the fear of the black beneath the white shine and the pink gum and the slither of the snaking romantic quality that love evil live over ever never. The devil lived especially how exquisite, so the fantasy plays true.

See, the problem with the sports is it's too vanilla the way it's exalted and remembered. There needs to be a retrospective on the inferno that is the sports pillar. The pillar that governs all religious zeal into an all-encompassing order, this is how you play. Refer to our simulated models of history.

One game is enough, but you cannot just watch one, addict yourself to the moment and forget all the rest. As long as you know how to be willing to gamble after research, you become an investor. Fix the fight and the rush is catfished, hence, the gambling at your own house. Nothing to line, gambler take nothing.

Minerva's bloody whale needs a chance, and the human factor keeps it interesting. But that crackle of harlots, there was a story there. An Everett Shinn painting.

All these old thoughts of idealistic, young explorerhood, back to the old country, the barded beard with the hunter's attire and long breaths and steady steps with the occasional burst of bullet bars to bridge the silence and pay off the silence from lacking concept and form. It was high time for an excursion back to the wonder years. The cackle of harlots had a black tongue and tar to boot the fall of the revolution.

What these women would never know, oh the pangs of the testosterone fueled madness, beseech the tip drill as the foundation that balances the bell ringers.

Achievement of the Dream

Hogwash

"I'm enjoying the view." Alabaster foam emerged from the cracks. The cabal crossed the catwalk and descended earthbound. Today had a mythical notion.

"Any time one takes aerial flight, speed, devised by motion, forced, masses, accelerate the reference point."

Accordingly, there was an orgy. Not of a typical notion, moreso a hyperorgy. Nebular atrophy was distinctive defensive barriers against the Isos' intent. Consubstantial deficiencies, defunct of progressive study, were eliminated on a daily basis. This had the makings of a grand opening.

The locus was forever open. Really.

Impending Doom

The living room was dead. All the curtains were covered. All the windows were covered with curtains jagged with the shadows. Whatever dynamism the room was built for was now static. White walls were grey. The air was still as the breath held. There were also lots of guns. Spread on the coffee table were books burned, ashes and some tobacco. No butts.

Previously entombed, a black and white photo peeked from the bottom corner of the most visible book. A man's hand reached for the photo, breaking the silence. Just as he examined it, a loud shot bellowed and a loud thud from the fall followed with some more clanks and drips from the aftermath. The photo glided back and forth to float down to the table. The shaded figure grasped the photo and tucked it away in a side pocket. Calculated boot steps with gonglike resonance bolted before a door shut and a car started.

The blood kept spilling.

*　　*　　*

"You know that feeling when you tear off a scab and the blood flows out?"

"That feeling depends on the intention."

"It's like when the water breaks."

"Like from the womb?"

"Yes. Birth. That's the most gratifying experience. Layers are created to be cut."

"You're a bloody masochist."

"That is the human condition."

"You'd make an excellent comedian."

"The crying clown greater than or equal to the smiling."

"But is the smiler crying inside?"

"Depends on these bricks of cartridges and shells."

"Look, Odon. I know where you're going with this and let me just say, yes, I get it. You're right. I hear you. I see you ... Now, what I don't see is where we will put the bricks."

"Mr. Gorey, I'm just a few steps ahead of you. They're already in the duffel bag beneath your seat."

"Let's make this quick."

*　　*　　*

Reporting in the proper context, the situation that would play out hones in the recursive rendition of a collective memory, hence, the flashbacks, the rewind of the linear trajectory. The venue was the sun and the physical elements bent on its strength. Solar power. Schools of fish intermingled the tanked walls with unfulfilled decadence. Not—that they had not taken chances—but rather—they had not taken the proper chance. Been it as it was, requisite nervous triggers were not wielded at ordered intervals on any level. This distinguishing feature was dormant in 1 Isos to an implicit rhythm. Undercover synthetic coats masked a torso cavity made of regenerative capable acids and an instantaneous circulation.

Assigned Today

"Tradesmen." He had once been a carpenter, at the imposition of the movement join. Now, he traded synthetic lumbers via capsule. His freak exception. Cosmically satisfied. His planks contained care packages. They were extremely durable. Lifetime warranty, or thirty days free, or your money back. No one ever demanded moneys back because everyone kept it. What a success.

When Mammoth contacted him, immediate payment.

The Muck Bowl

"You do see ... now, you do not have to walk through the door. There is no door." Dieter's words out of an intercom at the car bar. Mats' fingers played and the black meshed with the white. His pupils continued their expansion and contraction as his hands fused with the keys, his thoughts with the print. The pace of his wordplay followed suit within the margins. The gas station had become an American bazaar hybrid, a warped descendant of the Midwest general store. A foreboding nature permeated the air, incense infused and spiced with the scent of aflame tobacco. Corn dogs, too. In this niche, only bulls and harlots could survive. Was the station just a cipher, an overt simplification? Where was he talking about, to whom? Dieter? Tara?

A brood of nefarious heretics snared with crumbling civilization only as censored caricatures akin to comic villains. Mountebanks scourged the back aisles doused in tiger grease and salt. The grease and salt kept away the flies. It also attracted the hounds. Salted and greased skins aroused the most carnal desires. The breath musk was unbearable. Even though, the bars, the hounds' incessant pantings still reached the Vet. He had once been called a name but The Vet was all he went by now. His pod was in the corner, nearest to the bathroom where you could flush in and out.

* * *

Footsteps followed through the hallway. Two bullish men proceeded to the cleanse. The final man straddled the hall and took a keen position at the entrance way.

Plastic covered the body. Then the goons rolled it over and over again, then tucked it in a sleeping bag derivative. Shoddy work. Fucking goons. Never left anything right. The smoking one leaning on the door frame grunted, pointed, and redirected their movements. They did not have to be clean. The point of impact was common knowledge to even a greenback cop. This was a stealth operation. There were more pressing matters at light. Body extracted from the sight, blood puddles on wood intact, and the door left a crack open—the essential signs of a struggle gone awry. This was to be one in many of a series. An agenda had to be upheld and these were the men who would orchestrate the remains. For what cause was irrelevant. They were goons. But the smoking one, he knew.

Leverage can be wielded large and by a man who reckons there is an opportunity in grasp. Gorey, the smoking one was such a man. Taller than the average, lean though built, and a face broads deemed abominable for its coldness and allure. His second skin comprised of mod-like renderings of a punk expired; jet-black creases on the sleeves, collar up and wrapped U-like about the cheek bones, and the tail seams covered by a leather beam. A watch of reverence, boots reminiscent of combat, and slacked cords. Lots of zippers and pockets, hidden and hiding. An aura of prominent antiheroism beamed.

He was the type to survey the environment prior to agreement to perform his work. His work consisted of deflecting truths in order to mask his clients' desires and accordingly direct their enemies to dead ends, ideally damaging dead ends. Clients had a typical makeup: wrinkled, rich, and raucous in nature. Bodyguard accompanied. Facades of eminent political attachments. Confirmed without. Certainty. These types had paid handsomely for his services. Revolving the circle, the going rate was only rising into orbit. So was the sun and with that, they were gone.

Mats had idealized the man, the Gorey grant. Wishes fulfilled.

Mr. Gorey was a harrower. Not by cause, but by effect. Had he been a carpenter, those outside of direct contact would be splintered. Collateral damage could be the only conclusion to this trade. You build it up, you have to tear it down. Just make sure you are covered by insurance.

By experience, the insidious course of events always played out the same. This particular client required a secret to be deemed necessarily secret, then necessarily exploited, spread and controlled. Only a man of Gorey's balls and qualifications could perform.

He had begun by admonishing the seekers and explicating the magnetic danger attached to their quest. Discovery of a secret, they so thought, is a power play. Coup d'état. So, they discussed components of the secret, played the secret field, and gained some knowledge of the secret. But to their dismay and relief, Gorey did not provide the answer. The given clues were not sufficient for the sum, and upon this realization, their motivations crumbled. Their mouths remained active, or their keyboards or their phone screens, so rumours ran rampant through the texts of the time. Ignorance fueled the clients' nefarious intentions.

Gorey continued the task, occasionally sought respite in the form of aged bourbon, menthol cigarettes, and dames of positive energy. On a night standard, she had came, touched, and went.

On a not so standard night, Mats shared the bottle of whiskey.

*   *   *

The forms were no longer visible. Neither were the hooves. Only the eyes. The Vet didn't need to show his face. He remained visible through the shards of broken mirrors arranged in a makeshift fashion, order from chaos over time, random walks to rest. Only through this reflected image could one notice the chaotic rage lurking behind the

crimson eye. Greyscale creases cut hid leather garb in a most violent
nature. Cowhide leather shielded him from the mask. It counteracted
the musk whenever the metallic merry-go-round rotated from their
side to his.

*   *   *

In exchange for body parts, anything from a toenail to an impaled
head, The Vet provided orders. He had misfortune cookies for the
early crowd. And the constants. The given ingredients were organic
in nature and the effects were phantasmal in result. Self was irrelevant. Isos morphing into the squeeze, the vise grip of vicissitudes.
Your prime target, the addicts, they are the authority on these matters.

Third party shades intensified the blight of the warped fixtures.
Timing plays the ultimatum to experience. How shades clarified their
gas guzzling oblivion. Preoccupation with routine was the current
epidemic. Theirs was a flesh diet. The automatics were the going concern. Rise up. Cruise. Mirrors. Blind Sides. Wave running. With
sound speeds the standard. Systemic limitations had been extinct for
decades by now. "What was the matter?" A bit of absurdity surely
owed its merit to sharp memory. Moments of such had transgressed
from present through to expectation. Free fall. What an oxymoron.

Push and Pull Tactics

The drags on his cigarettes were like those breaths a bull takes after a prolonged heat. "Sure, I would kill everyone if they were not already beyond death. It's a state so morbid," The Virus beseeched The Vet to respond, even a knuckle crack or a hawk of a spit ball. Nada. "The drones go to and fro but never project out of the plane. They're soldiers with no commanders. Cars with no drivers. It ceases to be a car then. Players with no captains. No longer players. Or better yet, conscious beings overdosed on consciousness without a God to keep them in check. Fuck that God concept, it's a figment. I'm all for the energy and the sounds of the universe but any culpable cerebral being that resides in the aether is an earth-launched concept."

"Where is my shoelace?" Echoes of the Half Dome.

"I'd consider astral projection as my next program on the virtual landscape."

Distraction. Attraction. They, these heiresses had an antiquated strut and meditated approach. Somewhat comfort in a seminal nomadic way. She, in this particular, had that runway gait. Runway form. Universal face. An ideal rendition. Skin like the ocean. His dick really rode her visual tide. Disengaged, there was no orgy.

Calm the circles.

Extraction points.

Nothing was a bother. They did not need mirrors. Shards of the whole emerged in harmony. To a fugue state. Constant strange looping disintegrated the extensive barriers to a subliminal waypoint. Aquatic portals were frozen stable. Gurus jettisoned through swinging ships to render time secondary to predatory meditation.

They'd gaze ghostly. She dreamed. Both were dazed to some unfathomable common ground, explicated by its lack. Virtuous indifference permeated the scape. Upon these realizations was a slacking calm, tranquil to an eerie placidity. The novels, zines, films, albums, all lined the walls as replenished spores on a sponge. Shared scapes created an island beyond a mired subjective consciousness. Reef hedges, endocrine and exo-, accounted for the analog visualizer.

"Such folly."

"Banter is endearing."

"How dare you."

"Blow me."

Nautical Treads

Vehicular mayhem composed the beat of the day. It had been a company car. Technically, it still was but technically, there was no record. Statute of limitations. Smearing trash was one of The Vet's hobbies. It was a peaceful exercise. Entropy in a controlled space elucidates an authentic pleasure. Of course, augmented neurotransmitters initialized the senses. Other than kitschy pornography, this habitual activity morphed into a manifest smorgasbord of material. Elementally derived waste can be recycled, recomposted, reused, and cycled again and again. A natural pool, Infinite looping engages the gambler. Recursive moments for the man diversified his memory bank. Wielding the brain had become manual, auto-levels, lights, ledgers extinguished on that conscious tip. So much waste a dust bag could never gather.

*   *   *

Crescendos of horror, her voice oscillating between cracks of glass and the metronome of an arrhythmic heart. Carrying was the only option for the fine man. Hell, Daisy Presto could eviscerate Grecian amphitheatres of a solvent interest. Auditory measures failed to express her succubus nature.

Derelict marble coated the floors. Distressed were the cracks in the tiles. Saving her was the score. Actually, it was the game. Survival was relative.

Stereo waves, the truth of false prophets. The source code was in his fiber. Colloquial dynamism created everlasting banter, associates street hoodlums common to vehicular mayhem.

Inverted Cataracts

"You don't say?"
"I do. Man, that veracity is yet to be matched."
Ah ha ha ha ... such a painstaker. Boy, they come and go.
Timing is always the issue.
So she had said.

She was right.
You'll find another version.

Facial recognition cursed into his memory. Photographics had debunked his myths. But now, occupational hazards bogged the waking dream. Kneelers twisted the endless hallways. The attendees were auditory in majority. Seeing was not believing. Necessarily, they were all blinded. Upon entrance, eyesight was censored and regulated by the Isos. Cosmic auditory augmentation enabled them to experience waves through a polygonal deconstructive mechanism, synonymous with allegorical composition.

"You can choose two roads. They run parallel, side by side, but there are multiple waypoints. The way of death and the way of life, bad, good, what have you, but I like that seeing greyscale, enough with the poles and the ying yang balancing act. Crossover is inevitable."

"I think we're all shot out of the cannon and wherever you land, you splatter."

"Pollination. Precisely."

"Not a bother."

Trials

The derelict bastion leaned dry. Castilian hubs ascended the gunners. The lingering miasma stung the air. Heavy barrels, now empty, tops off, were scattered amongst the dust. To be brief, there was no dust. Permeating the layers of smog was the humanoid mass, the orifice of a conscious tip. Mind flows were habitual in this context. Only a true and tried Lab Rat could handle the setting.

Nevertheless, obviously present were the skags of youth, flawless superficial and deathly at the epicenter. Sure they may have been dames of classic science but no more or less cogs in the grand scope of a paternal society.

"Spoken as a devout misanthrope," Pierrou declared.

"And the point being?"

"Your walls don't even lean."

"Point taken. Why don't you refer to your DSM-8 or -9, robotic and calculated for the masses." Pierrou raised the finger and that was that.

However, the night would enfold, the comrades' scape had an enthusiastic glow to the horizon. Odds were the scallywags and base fiends would end up in their proper destinations of convention, but perhaps, there were an off-the-beat few that could grasp the true experience of a singular plane.

Cascading beams of high frequency lights stung the crowd's eyes. They had no concern, for the sounds overrode the vicious eyescapes. Harrowing the visual mine field were not only these dexterous kaleidoscopes of color but also that cherry blossom curvature of a fine humanoid coke bottle, upper or lower however you calibrated your looking glass. You got to be on an observatory grind in these games. Never fully into the motions but always treading the thin ice cake.

At this point, I was bored, I sought a pedantic connection. Logic holds that I could just go call the trap residents of Cherry Street and transition my post-hedonistic trip into the spiraling caverns of apathy, yet tonight was one of those where the environmental scents harped toward an orgasmic temporary conclusion.

Actuaries

Ohms of ohms elucidate this situation. Barriers are eradicated as fast as they are constructed. So much toil among those that don't need it. These heiresses had an antiquated strut and a meditated approach. Extraction points. To the cool breeze.

Nature Nurture

Mats had lost his cool. He needed structure. Old granularities mix mashing back into recall. Names, faces, voices, ghosts, ghouls of damned transgression. Sell your soul, eat a cupcake, erase the path. This had happened before, the disorientation upon fortuitous happenstance. Never in such grand amenities. Granted, no options were present to vest, his tenure short term, though maximizing his earnings potential via the development of the Isos phenomenon. He had never vocalized it, and he still did not want to hear an auditory expression of those taboo words to get her stripping his cerebellum like a Big Brother poster. Constant, unassuming, alarming, totalitarian assurance.

Then, he remembered because a shoulder invasion took place, and a drag and a merry banter through the strobing lights and the leopard poolskin felt and the Homer Simpson on a dumpster sticker marking the score for the darts whizzing by the Tyrannosaurus Rex headpiece over the brick and mortar fireplace. They entered, shoved in by the Burlik demolisher, and familiar specters became alive through the smoke and the tungsten vinegar light.

Gorey, the great chimera, at his right hand, Meyer, at his left foot, Alexey, and at center back-seat, the Lucifer spawn himself, Sir Virile The Vet. Motley possums with obsessive compulsions for subversion and vagina pillage. They all had specific chambers to conduct their affairs. In this theme, the back bar, it had to be for convenience and a pleasant reinitiation to ignite my drive to join back with the old band, sensible though insidious. Who could trust these sketch sacs? I sure as hell couldn't, considered Mats, they'll probably try to call me Higgins and propose another quick haberdash and take my country dream and remix it to a pagan ceremony for hair shaving, rug burning, and jizzing into soda bowls. So much for remaining off the degenerate grid. See, the thing was, staring into those eyes, all of them might as well have laser beams with omniscient narrative vision, prodding into the black vessels streaming with nitrous-fueled blood, and collectively, concentrating on the man in the doorframe, brights flashing until he relented. It was fact.

They knew. And it was time to collect.

Cerebral Goretex

The beta had no side effects. Listed was blank. Abrasive rushes of shackling tension. Flashbacks, craters created every time the brain received a corrupt transmission. His nerves were a wreck. Well, you become your own guinea pig, things will get hairy. All for the money, all for the freedom. Survival critical, then the open road to the sea of lore. He had hairpins now. By previous names, he still called them. That was when they referred to him as Higgins. Insider operations were insider operations for a reason. Because names were arbitrary and faces and voices were all premeditated.

See, now, subversion had penetrated the system. Revolution was replaced with conspiracy. Ramifications destructive, in what capacity, to be determined upon conclusive evidence staging a bottleneck, crisis, focusing event, concurrent strategy execution to follow. The outcome all but guaranteed: dent the wall.

Wall Flowers

Glitches, blemishes, where logic took a nap. The wall had many names, institutional, ideological, dogmatic. The record held, and these asterisks were noted. They together could not be added and combined, just the way percentages are independent, mutual exclusion. So, the media puppets had their paychecks to confabulate a theory and a tabloid of recycled thinking for the circle masturbation. Duck, Duck, Goose on my Gooch. The asterisk had to be more than asterisk. And my genetic makeup sat on the brink where the rolling stone could amass in finite tentacles until tangling and knotting into concrete-hull layers malleable to every direction and cardinal plane sensibility. Why could it be so coincidental? Because it wasn't, because even if your shit gets flushed down the toilet, it still goes somewhere, just out of sight and smell. And when it comes back in your drinking water, you have to drink up. Energy cannot be created or destroyed.

Mine could be copied. Counterfeit equivocated to new serial numbers. Let the reserve print the new bills. The click of a button. I hadn't signed off all my rights. I had shares. They wanted some sharing.

The Leaning Mast

Gorey prepared the memo. He always came prepared. What a perfunctory conductor. He could sell the Torah to Islamic militants and not only that, he could get them to push it like smack and cheese. All the work was already done, I just had to sign and mail it in. We'd do this together, he had said. He had also used the word 'behoove' to formally request the task to completion require his direct supervision. I'd get something out of this, too, and it wasn't karma he was advocating. It was strategic consultation. He already knew where I was heading, claiming this is why he had swooped me under his wing into the careening speedboat of influence and purposeful subterfuge and guerrilla espionage. Because I had class, as far as fighting without my hands went, that my brain was a pitbull juiced up with the golden bough of hammerhead shark instinct and bodhisavatta resolve. I was too young for wisdom. Even if I had it possessed, it served better to keep it to myself. East Broadway suspended sickly in the cloudless night and the passing breezes were reminiscent of breaths a dirtbag releases after a three-day bender lacking toothpaste and gag reflex. We were almost there.

The post office was closed. How imaginative suitable that some act of true terror could be conducted at such a locale. The post office is the most underutilized, neglected, adopted son of the government family. Unappreciated, unrecognized, and unfathomable in comprehension. For what can truly go on through all that circulation. Exploitation just needed a nudge. I had a supreme nudge in Gorey. No fear, just it had to be this way. They wouldn't bother me. Gorey just wanted to be on the board of directors. What a crack pot.

Jizz Maze

They had surveillance. They knew more than Mats. He did not try to hide this. It was obvious from the start. They just liked playing out the development like a movie. Gorey was always a sucker for Jimmy Stewart, Hitchcocks. For the sap could be transmogrified into a laminated simulacrum of actualized, cinematic heroics. Here and behold, I was the rescue rod, the singularity share, the white buffalo impregnating Europa with my capsule-converted content. It scared me that the disruption to the social-nuclear family order had a monetary impact that was already turning psychological. For, now, the survival of the fittest was eradicated. If every mope and mopette could inject orgasmic talent, then talent ceased to be. Skill was nullified. The consequences were self-culpable. But Wooly's stock was rising and there was a split.

Tiger Tails

Hallways, subterranean, seedy green light, tiles of turgid bowel and bile resin rising. Did anyone notice the detergent, cleaning products sweeping, marauding as solvents for ossified shit, as it were a whole steady constant that upon the wear and tear of the standard metropolitan grind, there is a certain threshold reached and you just never can come back from that. Unless of course, proper makeover, substitution, plastic, all for the sake of beauty. Akin to the senses the way a white tee shirt is never again its origin color after a few wear and tears through the carcass of a downtown enterprise.

Here and behold, the rat corridors had new advertisements. The drugs were hitting the market, with the insignia of legitimacy, and oh but surely, were there fortunes, subpoenaed to trustworthy money managers and hungry hungry holders of share. Mats started feeling mopey, almost embarrassed, as if the ads were calling him out, like they knew it was him, and they were Big Brother reminders. You make your money with a smile, you can be sure we know, even though we don't. White teeth, glistening makeups, thumbs up, let's celebrate. And the next ad, the quintessential cool clique drinking some whiskey that swallows popularity because prestige has already been emptied and saturated upon reach. The walls are closed. Please, just open these doors so I can get out of here. Mats had a preordained commitment. A ball.

Adulation for the Jews

Had he ascended to adulthood? See, where parties are places where you get perspiration due to the lights and standing, without the conflagrations of rainbow variations and death burgeoning bass drums. These are gatherings, socially, constrained by pomp and class carryovers and carryforwards. Deals could be implanted here. So could her implants. She wanted him to nudge a feel.

Still, there were lots of eyes on him. Not that those eyes would care if he even grasped a full handful. His hand could not cover that surface area. What bulbous proportion to that sliver of a waist. Now, no latex, just velvet, and fur. Like there was a difference. This is where the sweat came in. He imagined Ophüls' flowful camera weaving his life into the opera of the human comedy and how here, Lothario, here was where he could make declarations. He had quite a large account in his name, at the time. Confidence, exuberance, wield the flame of American zest for all its propaganda and might. It's good to be versed in foreign cultures in America, as long as you showcase a proper familiarity and recognition. No one gives a shit about respect, just recognition. What a dung hole. God, Mats had to love it. The fallacy. See, here and behold, he so said to himself, probably the tenth time on the hour, he was still an American but he had had his experience in European theatre. A proven experience, screw the showcase sophistry. But, see, he sought some sexual enterprise. He had some insiders do the whisper rounds, and so they knew, now, he was the Source Code. Would they care to take a load down and up, and maybe exchange data? It was so sterile, the vernacular. Good thing this wasn't a silicon valley. Vomit.

Vaudeville Waterworks

Had it been a sideshow? The perpetual hallucination shared with witnessing pretenders, or rather, more inclusive, willing participants in the pre-flood chaos. Stepping out to balconies is the sanest motion to make at these sorts of fart conventions, other than the walk of the exile, to leave, leave, never more, and flurry onto a broken boulevard to get a quick blowey and swallow semantics through pizza. He had to be here, not for a speech, but for politics.

That savory word, politique, la stratégie des maîtres, deux fautes. See, the following week, the major publications were to unveil their campaign awards, awards recognizing the pettiness of their own backers. Centripetal forces allow for the circle jerk to gain such momentum that you're stuck to the walls, you can't tell direction, your eyes and ears are subjugated to the rotations until they're so fast and constant you can't seem to get a personal bearing. Just ride the wave, dig in, we got wax for your digression.

Balcony was even better because he was a prime target. He had trailers. They battled between themselves. They agreed for tag team action. Two on one. Their names were Henrietta and Rosalyn. English *troff*. High grade. Expiration dates not for twenty years, hands down. Contenders for certain crowns, the night's open one, no doubts or qualms for even sober sissy. They exchanged number codes, and drinks were to follow, when the promontory rider of the revolution emerged from the shadow, a wraith in wigged disguise, so fitting that what he typically presented was more the disguise.

Gorey had pertinent information. There'd been some shocks to the valves and because the piping had very old reinforcements, the faith had been overcast. The board was no longer the destination. For a trust had been established, mortgage security was backing these envelopes that held property tags and henceforth, large investments would be made through a brokerage house that had a special relation with a pardonable underwriter initially valuing in the hundreds of millions. A score unseen and unsavory for a grunt on the ground, but when it came to Gorey, this was propaganda's gateway to the future paradigm. Revolve the fascists around revolutionary sublimination and what have you, the society would suspectedly collapse in on itself until the fascists were revolutionaries and they would never be the least bit aware of their treachery to their coda and schema and flora and fauna, like church, dockers, and dismissing art house crackpot liberals with large bank accounts and low grade balls, would revert to proto-fascists on Prozac and would start really backing their leaders who believed in change and being poster boys for rock star ideologies that could only be fulfilled by second rate bullshit sprinkled with some large words that were easy to learn and repeat and by a few smirks of mirthful omniscience.

To instill the cycle of teach and take, Gorey just wanted shares, once the virus was released, it would take a course of its own. Mats had just wanted all this bullshit to be cut away. The cake looked like fecal matter from his naïveté. Lots of sleep required, after his head nods, his agreements, his actions were immutable, they already so in place, yet why would Gorey be absorbing his worries and delineating his inner monologue to be tracked by Mats and his concurrent relation to the methodologies being headsprung and expediently conducted, interfaced by platforms preprogrammed? Was it that he was the plutonium, that he had to be M & A, A & R, S & M, to utmost care and supervision. Come monitoring, come Big Brother, come the perks of the postal rewards. The letter was already delivered. He'd be getting on the board. Mats already knew, to protect his identity, he'd pull a fast one and unveil a GQ-rendered Gorey crossed with Dos Equis sensibility and thereby, mystère the board under a veneer of ubiquitous somnambulism. Puppets could be perfunctory.

They were clearly on cameras now. Not that it mattered but at core base, we are men and this is an eternal struggle, we are assimilated into the machine immense. Immense and loathsome, recognize the need to disrupt the cataracts. Jam the sockets. Gorey was such a drama king.

He was in disguise, they were drunk patrons at a social bloodbath. No one knew anything. Mats saw the flutter of legs and longings and walked off. He accepted his position. He was incorrigible, they were going to follow him, they were going to force compliance, and coercion was a banned word for an agent double entwined.

Cunt's Coincidence

Heaps on heaps of hellacious flesh. Flesh over the hip, flesh over the heart, under the skin. It was igniting, the double dose of energizer bunnies to fuel the flame of the holy orgasm. Henrietta and Rosalyn were twin post-debutante neo-goalkeepers. They had been prep school rivals, both collegiate successes, and alternated their champion post bilaterally, at first, until Rosalyn's two-time repeat come the junior to post-senior year. By that time, Henrietta had graduated early and been commandeered by the demagogues of metropolitan industry, specifically, the garmenteers and garment seers who besought her fit for runway conduction and concurrent brand mobility. She had harangues of influence for indirect purposes, associations so haphazard one's wont to declare proper indicators for profitability would require theoretical discussion and the insidious sway of the image-media lottery.

Granted, she was sponsored, she was a face, and she kept it up with utmost care and contempt. Hence, the cocaine. Double edged swords were defunct, for the shotgun buckshots to the nostrils, she had devised a new sing. It involved an invention of her own deviation from the relational norm. These co-pilots thought it cute to snort with large denominations and ironic corporate coffee house straws, not to mention the color gradations of the nails, symbolic of primal screams and slumbers. She was a writer for the blind anonymity of the projection screens, and she catered to this audience by circumventing such banal instruments as the pen and the quill for the glow of the sterility screen and the plastic seduction of alphabetized keys. Hence, what use for these pens once they were obsolete. Obsolescence involved innovation. Revolt, reinvention, a rewind to relapse forward over the bullet train. And here and she beheld, the dual-pronged pen apparatus required for incision. Double play pen. They could get used to this.

Washing Machines

A cool beach had litter sprinkled on the sensuous sands while the howl of a battleship lurked as the beacon for storms imminent, queued in the meteorological cycle yet conceived by the conscious colony. Hence, the beachgoers had already arrived, set up makeshift belvederes, verandas, teepees, towelettes, crèmes, fragrances, salt-infused, only organic and cared for with the sands and the waters in mind, because God forgive, she wore a fur and there are no excuses for environmental neglect, rape, and pillage. Thing is, the portable barbecue, propane, salacious fumes to the sky, this was the focal point distracting the head-on from succumbing to the sand between the toes. He carried on, vertiginous, because he just could not feel his toes since he had not gone to the sands. He remained concrete-bound, leather-bound in stocky sandals, lots of hair winding in the invisible-moon swayed tide, seagulls lurching over the castor cloud forerunning the battleship and the gathering wormhole of a hurricane on the horizon. He descended the steps, circumventing the artifice. For, now, it was an apparition, the waves, the tide, the natural courses, for they were in a tank, where were the cameras? Henrietta shone bronze like a buttery wonderful dough formulated into arduous geology. A frisbee shamrocked her head, they were frozen, and her form dissipated into molten nothing, and the red horcrux of the frisbee Jim Beamed onto the gravitational course to hit the steps just as he descended passed eye range to the sloping surface of the sanded fabric.

Specter number sighting two of Henrietta was mistaken. It was another form, another shade, another hairmonger with appetizing attraction. She curtailed her angelic beams into the water and saturated overdrive resulted in flux capacity incision. In other terms, the stairs would have been the righteous decision. Yet, being that this was a dream and the visual viewpoints were quite scattergrammed, like a histogram with gaps in the lines between the bars, things were best put as edged-out greyscales. Looked at and beheld, the stairs were merging into a ramp, the sands were creating temple pillars of gathering weight and domino effects scheduled for collateral damages, and upon realization, terror strikes minor chords. The water bowl took precedence over the sands swallowed and sublimated into the magical splendor of saltwater onto concrete, and the wipeout was cancelled out by the initial charge of vertigo for the habitual delight in self-aware dreams. Tanks always sprung leaks. Time told the reset, the storm hit the sound of the squawk of the crying gulls and awake cast Mats into a myopic elucidation that a true pleasure it was to gain Cartesian consciousness via eight accompanying limbs instead of four, independent of his extension. Blood noodles. A red-entombed Louis Vuitton mobile marker. Cosmology, sorcery, where does it end, if there are no cords and invulnerable batteries. Components drive chaos. Cigarette recycled reboot. Hello sunshine.

Of Gods and Monsters

"What do you want to know about whales?"

Silence.

Muffled farts under breaths receded.

"Ok, moving on. Let's recall Perseus and the Medusa to slay."

Gonads were sore, first thought upon sobriety. They were clean, surely, fine upstanding coquetry aside, they were clean. They had to be. Such fine construction and comfort. Associative assumptions aside, and the gaping abyss where Yes and No meet, one chooses to show the goods, while the other may know Yes is lying at No's amusement, and Yes knows more of how to keep the adventure astream astringent aside from No's serious incursions. Losing sight of the opposites, the ultra loss for Mats had been quite engaging. Two chicks at the same time, let's mark that one notch noteworthy among a myriad canvas of gubernatorial gaudiness and accomplished vigor. Vigaro, Figaro, wield the monopoly board, you're packing Thunder. Meat Heat on Prime Supremacy. Isos, sharing, copying, replicating, imitating, negating, nullifying, conforming. He had no role now that his stream came copied and carefully screened by the federal forces for approval, safety, over the counter was imminent, this was just the start. Could he take pussy in square, 2 power 4 power 16. He'd set himself goals. But Gorey kept prodding about the corporate caverns. Mats took the week off. He had missions.

Objective: Get away from oneself.

Root-Access Point Perseus

"You are a lucky devil, if I ever knew how to properly read the Book."

Smug was the smile lost to the smirk shared by the violenteers.

The Forging of the Tarantula

Headlines spectacular in dramatic irony. For, what better way to escape than to cut off the personal distribution. No radio, non waves percolating through invisible gateways, especially windshield that glistened so transparent in its objective design. The rental was a loaner that was borrowed via the vertical structure that seamlessly ensconced harmony and hegemony, all hail the new kid on the block, Isos was a keeper!

The city ruckus nefariously assuaged Mats that he was a singularity, already beyond the horizon, where the horizon was no longer a horizon, where it was just an amoebic mass space closed off by limited human capital constraints. Exemplary by the three dimensional mundanity and the meandering dead end stump of oh, look at me, I'm a star child and my primary function is to be the object of your fantasies. Hence, the floating, in a semipermeable bubble, visible to outsiders, yet the cosmic controls had specific coordinates and ulterior motives carry with them subterranean intentions and contingent outcomes of critical mass can sputter and lurch onto ignorant collaterals like viruses to petty hemoglobes.

Gorey pestered the technological fronts. Good things batteries still had half lives. They were all expired, moreso, disconnected, to be obnoxious plastic blocks that clapped up and down along the bumps of the road, a primal domino effect, Mats was driving fast. This was a loaner. He best not forget, abuse is encouraged. Disclaimed, enjoy your freedom to destroy someone else's capital cretinous urn.

He had trouble losing sight of the road as the sun descended behind amorphous green clouds coalescing with the dusty entrails of manufactured wastes gaseous and halcyon-primed. This was across the riverway through the trees and the piss-infested water fountains and tangibly corrupt-systemic deficiencies poaching the waterways with cluttery contempt for longings long sedated lying dormant in the stigmatized minds of the laborers who played security. When there are no threats, there cannot be any more dreams. Mats looked aghast, the radio from leaking border riders and drivers, invading his enclosed shell of temporal bliss. Isos advertised, even the rock and roll stations were gathering followers. Like waterboarded slow talkers, a single droplet metronoming the room, the shell, the road, he heard hiss remarks and burning laughter and considerable merriment at agreements upon the possibility of sexual adventure rekindled, all in the safe-sterile form of Isos released to the market. The BMW teal to the right had a couplet, one heaving up and down, the other chin cocked back in ecstatic relief, and the Isos commercial, all in triad major, diminished by the faint tint and the descending disappearing sun against the green-hued waste clouds, and at least come traffic, there could be ethereal orgasm for one lucky specter. The sight admonished Mats, an omen of inescapability. He was amazed at the maze, and now that it had been a few days since Gorey's last successful contact, he feared perhaps the trial pills were setting him up for triage. He needed to get out. For no good reason other than his own peace of mind in the perpetual battle of conscious cannibalism. Kill one thought, build one more, it swallows another, and rewind to sleep, at least he had two chicks at the same time and he had yet to dream what dreams would prosper and show forth upon sober sleep on a cabin night not far off, on passed the sight of road and trees, and no concrete mirrors riddling the way rear. When he could really breathe and really be one with the Monks of old and seek enlightenment upon asking for forgiveness that was never going to come from anybody but himself. And the Isos. The Isolate, the Isos.

Fast Forward. Jump Cut. Flash. The night, the warm comfort of tint galore and distance refracted by the gradient shift to black. He discharged a few capsules from his go-go box, it looked like a microsafe only there was no place to combinate possibility. It functioned open and close via thumb print reader, like a nitrogen capsule, only more sleek and bleeding edge. Prototype, credit Dieter, these were definite, guarantors of chill out somber tones. He had really gotten used to putting up a chaotic medley to circumvent boredom's clutches and reverb into residual waves of diminishing returns of prodding hokey-tidbit lackadaisical chuckles and blotters of nuisance upon spotting his gaggy eyes in the mirror, as if he was penetrating the truth and the beyond the truth that only entailed darkness and a peace in accepting the nihilistic root of his experience as the Meant to Be. See, so much smoke up the ass has to have consequences, regardless of the flush out, the vacuuming, the rehabilitation and cleansing of the cavity. There are remnants, however beyond measurability. Intangibles are merely the limits to technology. But we keep on chugging ahead. And behold, the road opened upon the downcast of darkness and the pattern on the windshield showed signs never displayed in the sun, perhaps a sneeze that leaked excretion, hounded by a layer of bilateral musk and past cigarette smoke secreting dust particles. Very well, a ghoulish layer of blob slightly yellow under the tungsten roadlight, like an oversized over-easy egg, and then at the focal point above the steering wheel as base, a great firework motion of cathedral stringcourses. Pillars extending from a central brain, in all directions, as if a giant boulder rolled and pillaged and eviscerated all in its wake as a tornado, twisted yet accepting of all, encouraging all to join, along for the ride, the momentum, carrying forth, as the stability of being in the same place in a perpetual secondary motion carries traction, never friction, and only a footprint of never touching down.

It'd be soothing to go to space, if you could drive there, Mats considered. He stopped off at the gas station. He needed smokes, he called his voicemail, hung up before it connected. He had to be one hundred percent committed, if he wanted to ever reach some return to a base Chill. He was too hot, sweat glands emitting grease and nervous predilections upon entry to the bright lit, tiled to disgust, cornerstore of American capital tradition.

He got himself an Icee, a to-go insta-coffee, the smokes that required smoking, and the concurrent matches and lifesavers because they had a positive spirit and taste and variability in flavor while maintaining a primal consistency.

Flashes of warlocks sputtering down the road. A van without proper exhaust, more smoke, a rescinded muffle, Harley Davidson, gulags of futuro bikers with streamlined leather and stunt drives. This was a good stretch.

There was no way he could know they were following him. He accepted they always had been, they always would be, and now upon greater preferred shareholder stock, his freedom eliminated at security's wealthy expense. This was a good, good, nice stretch of American road, and the city was just a memory he'd cycle back to like the moon at conclusion of a cycle around the orbital office cerebrum.

The Land of the Judges

The board hordes had delineated Mats equipped and debriefed for vacation. This was the crux. See, he had quite an insidious foray in pleasurable whims whirled into a pool of drowning odious impiety. Simple summations, simple outcomes. Animalistic overtake.

Coverage. Media. Money.

Now, bad news turned good. Control is the Converge.

Hence, Vacation delineation. Holiday, perpetual until contract expiration. What satellite destination beholds the least risk for the company while also pressing matters to his climate-controlled independence. If he goes, it's not such a bad thing, now is it?

Dieter spoke slow, "you can burn the bridges, but not the bridge builder. It's bad for morale."

Guffaws. Cigars. Roosters.

The Outpost of Flames

The kaleidoscope of sunlight reaches all cardinal points in the cloistered hexagons of grass and stony embankment demarcated by doric columns, gargoyles of yester fable, and steeples of arcane might. Health augments the longing for the light to carry through the windows, that could be stained clear and the rotary tangents of reflections polarized strikes tides steady and somber in the construct of life gone from a city turmoil. Monastic tendencies are insidious upon such suburban design.

Following the cloisters, one returns to the courtyard for the parked all-terrain vehicles, four-wheeled go-karts, two-wheeled shockwave motorbikes, vibrant in color and aggressive purpose, a jeep caravan with no doors, a British relic of luxuriant off-road cachet, and the undercover standard four-door for runs to the grocery and supply quarry. With the cloisters separate by the courtyard for cars dormant, one enters the cupola enraptured with slanted slits for light that wrap around cylindrical to not only highlight but moreso envelop the form upon which the rays take shape in a spiral to the central stair, schismed by the reflectory tunnel for the noon light, to careen into a concentrated beam streaking down the portal into the living quarters of mystèred antiquity.

Another notion, another magical potency to play the daily game of preoccupation with self-infused isolation. It feels good, a bit undisciplined, though Mats had visited scheduled to pay homage to his uncanny state of affairs and the impending realization that this is a temporal haven. Enjoy it while it lasts, and share the spoils. Not for karma, just for pure hedonistic jolly-good-fun and a devil-may-never-care attitude about the denial of the semantic ownership of a Wooly

Mammoth corporate regime expediting rewards for the tax benefits. With the lowest common denominator adhered to in such paranoia, one cannot help but contemplate the other side of the coin: the darkened cooling metal, blocked from all shadow and spectacle, self-flagellant in its de facto state of insurmountable oblivion, pointed down, no basis for direction, no basis for perspective, only the great black void to swallow all possible trains of portent and prima donna drives.

Being as they are to be in the light, the flip side, the temptation to dictate the possibility of leakage, of a hole severing the oblivious void from the chaotic stage light, Mats considers that with a connection to the black, the unknown, the doom of it all building, he sees a permanent gateway, as if the flood has transformed the terrain and now, waves of tangible bodies to follow the gargantuan might of neon, semi-transparent representations of intangible conceptions. Specifically, why all the perks unless there is a remote choice festooned into a healthy soil that can grow and sprout into a more probable demise for said receptor, Mats, in the construct of the corporate labyrinth. They must have so much insurance on the place, and though those security cameras nestled into corners and crevices seethed in shadows as not to be obnoxious or conspicuous, they remain there, the security mainframe door is locked, perpetual power with backup generators not even needed for use, yet but maybe, there are already servers and connections transmitting to forces at work paying minions to record, observe, and communicate the behavioral modifications of a savage seed given free reign amongst a former tobacco baron's lair of power and profit. It's good to act like a king, for a day, for a month, for a few years, just as long as that contract expires and the payout clears all caveats for conflicts.

Keeping up airs in such a conundrum requires fortitude, mental striking of weights and control of said motions up and down, steady in place, free fall exemptions. The first visitation paid scheduled occurred on what would be Day 50. Two week buffer zone to prepare proper perceptions to be perceived, communicated, natural, unthinking, as if what could occur was to chance's whim rather than tactic's decisive hand. Assertion aside, a steady stream of piledrives had engaged Mats to put his embarrassment to proper use and once he had mined their deep, moist tunnels, they left heirlooms, souvenirs of said conquest, for he was the causal center piece for any female dream enacted to the flesh. The irony, he didn't even shave his balls anymore. They probably kept a lone pubiscus in a diary for that one time, in the land of the savages at the outpost of tantric denouncements, she had sailed on sublime waters above head, through misty clouds, seeking doomsday to come and acceptance of all the flux future held for the sake of Aphrodite's satiation. Their rations, they took with utmost professionalism, even gratitude, thank yous kept popping up via deliverymen absent, only indicative by packages left scattered amongst the estate grounds. The first, a box of foreign-born candies, taffies, fruit gummis, then came the white bread, and following a pause or a day of rest with no outside excursions, the rental car would unveil a package of vintage audio discs, swing music, bebop, jazz, the soul of the dream kept outcast and singular denoted a niche where the universal held it should be the loudspeaker focus. After the ultimate test, the Boss had come, in the form of adult pornographer Layla, and he had aced, all instances of the spectrum, the bell curve from one attractive tremor to the finality, had demolished the Temple, on a figurative basis. He had done his duty, his seed was cataclysmic, but he should put it to proper use.

Determinations called for vanishing, disappearing, erasing of the distribution. First and foremost, how could one incite sabotage. The simulacrum was already in full fledged capacity production, manufactured via robot hands, recursively twisting components blind to the naked eye into bite-size treats, then reverbed into plastic sterile compartments, then tagged together and wrapped in paper instruction and boxed guaranteed pleasure.

Isos was a simple design, a white box, red lettering, not much different than a care package from the Red Cross. Only the cross was an X and it seemed to revolve around a silver border that merged with the classic typographic impact of the streaking font Veranda playing Isos.

"Why would I have my own product?"

"Donate to the masses."

"You call yourself a part of the masses."

"Well, it's a matter of displacement. For instance, via travel, a stop in the country, one would hope, now wouldn't anyone hope, upon such an exclusive invitation to exclusive party, primal in demand, there'd be a gift to mark the moment, tangible, so upon return to the masses, there would be an item to signify the moment, to make it real to the spectators and the listeners."

"You see, young man, she clearly has a penchant for orating to the Eastside crowd. She likes being a talking head, and she wants proof."

"She should just film it."

"Like they aren't already doing that?"

Chuckles. The wide-bellied Bunalti had raised his corpulence off the couch and to the desk riddled with half-full liquor, he targeted the scotch, harrowed a pour, guzzled a light one, and clacked the ice into the amber potion for another theoretical postulate. "Once you accept the possibility of the worse already being the worst, that it's not a question of when or how or why, it becomes a question of triggers. Destroy your defense mechanisms. Hyperawareness. Once it's de facto you're being watched, this is being recorded, it's the natural state of affairs, then you can embrace your personal freedom. What remains private is your thoughts, your internal strife, and anything you choose to broadcast, well, it shall be noted. You are guaranteed as a participant in the making of the history, now, how great a role you choose to play, that's still fortune and chance together down a random walk of forking paths."

"Like how you have come here."

"Is that right?" Mats said just to prove he was listening. Not much of a proof.

A loud glimmer of discordant ah's and hmm's, for Lady Lois had arrived and marked her posse scatter through opposing doorways so she could take court independent, alone, opulent through the final penetration to the drawing room where Mats meditated, Lucretia fawned, and Gio Bunalti bustled his gourd ever splendid.

The embrace of pampered pussies. Mats' gaze striking Bunalti's stare, a murmur of "she should have been a singer," a shared sarcastic dose, the refraction of reflectory light across the crisscut pattern of doubleknit chamois and chambray skirts fluttering across the drawing room in the wake of poured mojitos. The clang of the gong, the transition to a piece by a contemporary artisanal trio from the gulags of the Northwest territory, recently featured in a retrospective at the Museum of Lost Art Found, entitled Nirvana for Hobos. Lots of distortion, heavy melodic syncopation, red-lining voices, losing oneself in the chord progressions, silence is platinum on the value scale, all for the sake of real emotional resonance. Until the questioning barrage.

"Who was the best?" inquired Bunalti. With the trio now a quartet, the sexes united on separate fronts until the inevitable parlay and renege into progressive gender roles, an erasure of preternatural pretense and prejudice. Henceforth, it was Bunalti interrogating Mats, the ladies off to the powder room, some evolution. If only they had cameras on them now, would they be performing even more cryptic and coy.

"That's an unanswerable."

"You're on the spot, just look at this place. Who's most enjoyable for a repeat?"

"That's a distractor."

"Share the wealth, friend."

"I should not be the source code for your sexual judgments."

"You've been granted a role, embrace it, encode it, wield it."

"There hasn't been much wielding."

"You fool."

"It's nice for the reserve tanks, I got it all right up here," gunshot finger to the temple, boom, "but it's not like I wake up, look in the mirror, and thereby associate my persona with the amply-put-to-use Johnson already awake below the equator."

"You have an exclusive experience, extremely rare in these times. Akin to a harem demand, supplied willingly, without transactional basis."

"That last part is total bullshit."

"That's not what I've been hearing."

"Let them have a fantasy, a pretense, I'm gonna come regardless."

"Exactly my point, when that's reciprocated, and they know it ahead of time, they just lose all inhibitions."

"They never have any."

"What does it go, again?"

"Riddler, joker ..."

"... shuffle the deck, the greatest trick the cunt ever pulled was convincing everyone it was under control."

"The devil knows otherwise."

"Think the timing should kick in."

"For what?"

"The song change, the interchange, if they stay in there any longer, the assumption is they're taking bilateral dumps."

"Don't demean the ladies with such ..."

"Unpleasantries."

"... raw images."

"Anyway, this isn't going to be an orgy. I'd shit myself than risk your naked carcass anywhere near my person."

"Tell me how you really feel."

"I'll only tell you how she really felt."

"Haha, you swine, you, what happens if this all goes away?"

"I'm still on the upward trajectory, the peak hasn't been cleared yet, and like all prudent investors, I'll have a ready-made hatch coordinated for escape if it comes to that point."

"It shall."

"It always does. How do you know I don't already have an idea?"

"Ideas are loose change, plans are small bills, actions are the treasure."

"You need to fix that, I want a more smooth saying payoff."

"I gather the rug under the crowd and then the superglue comes up through the weavework and they're stuck in place. You follow?"

"So you never have to pull the rug under, the point is to make them stick."

"This sounds all rather knotty, good thing I can count on you, my boy, to assure my deep seeded troubles."

"Ok, El Rey Denmark, sit on your throne and I'll get you another scotch."

Reconnaissance

The general store, lots of dead staring at headlines, quick pops for paper focus, what's hot, who's in, who's out, what's the personal conflict on the high school mainframe for the daily hopscotch. Here we go, in queue, in check, under fire, 20 rockets shelled for substitute toiletries, boom, sustained, next, 14 for two packs of cigarettes, a low blow, short, still standing, a 30-rack of canned beer, 24, the strongest strike point yet, jet fuel, a perfect target, stalemate, eviscerate, clatter, register, commerce, silence. Swiping is so boring. There's no feeling involved, some will say there's no nothing involved. Just a projected symbol arrangement on a screen. Boo-hoo.

Déjà vu all over again. That same white van parked next, do they just follow me everywhere? It's not even the mind, it's just, if they got a job to do, they could at least get me a coffee in the morning, we could share smokes on occasion, I get it, they're in it just as much as I am, on a daily toil and tribulation. Who's to judge, certainly not me ...

Still in line, the wrong line, should've gone to the automated one across the street at the megastore, but no, I consciously choose to go arcane old-school, expect the time to slow down. You need it, cool it, Mats, way too much riddle me this crooked cabinetry rubbing against edges transforming in that egg of a head. Shave your face once in a while, you look like a caveman. It's part of the appeal, the gut punch says aloud through the reflection in the deep ever conscious scanner instrument. The red beam, the explosion without the collateral damage. All translated through the interplanetary circuitry of the grid, the marks of black tectonic and isosceles, quadrangular, pillars, the tag beyond serial.

Boom, he got it. It's license plates, that's what the fugue has been striving to release. The compulsion for escape, the vacation, his denial, his great perspired wan, failing and diminishing in the feces of sponsorship, on overload, now mellowed out with all this open space and these open roads. A steady dirge of normality, a soothing calm and clean and anonymity to focus on the true work at hand, the discovery of the life force and the fulfillment of desires. Dreams don't exist anymore, except as parallel realities constructed out of a blender of memory and recall's recoiling machination. Just get high, stop dreaming, that's what the girl Bri had said when he had first lost his virginity, the lone lost orgasm. She never had it, she couldn't, there was no reaction. She was doing me a favor, it had to be, sowing the seed and what he was to become, Mats digressed, or maybe she was just feeling older at 24 than she deserved, and sought a true recognition of her feline powers, seducing the young boy, 16, for a stroll through the organic causeway of fears and tears and maybe, maybe, even if she did not penetrate the gates of hell, she felt it was enough to just go for a ride along on the way to demonic ecstasy, even if she was too specific to fit on the ride, she would be happy watching the young man get a taste for what it's like to reach the holy mountain, before blinking back to the pacifying calm of the post-calamity. The Lost Orgasm, I wonder where she is scurrying about on such a calm day, is it calm where she is, is she looking at the same kind of street, the different kinds of people, the air feeling the same misty comfort against the cheeks, is she wearing jeans, is she on a bender, does she still binge, does she look that way still, surely, supposedly, if you reach that hand of cards developmentally, she should be doing her utmost to maintain and cultivate that gravitas, but where am I now, oh, yes, one more stop prior to lift off.

Burlik tried to show up. He left a note, the door had been locked. Thank the ruckus of the night past. Scattergrams of fecund resin, residue, residual effects still curtailing the pungent sweat of tepid smoke and oversaturated rugs and leather seating vessels, not to mention the lipstick stained glasses, the glasses contaminant with butts of half-smoked said stained warriors left to drown, rather than fight the burning battle beyond exteriors. There was a teddy bear eradicated by knifeplay, cards with topless starlets vomited onto the coffee table at the centerpiece of the foremost cloister, lights remained dim though on succumbing to the steady rising of the sun to high noon time, and to top it all off, a polaroid camera for blackmail. Mats confiscated what was necessary and placed them all in a neat stack, bedside of the carcasses of fantasies excreted by exhaustion, pipes emptied, what a bore after the big wave. When the dream is fulfilled and the debasement of performance art takes on new meanings, semantically speaking, the orgasm dance of libido, then what comes next is a sedate sociopathy, a neglected word for explication of acceptance for the matters arbitrary and yet, so viscerally responsive to recall and emotion's cathartic reminders. Now that it was a weekday, he had long last lost track from the pre-binge social court to the current bonanza of bodily waste products recovering to relapse later. Good thing he woke early. He usually despised it, in the company of people, because one had to worry about disturbing their slumbers. This case, it was relief respite, for they were all so botched out in far off conscious cornucopias, that any immediate noise would hit an anesthetized eardrum or a misfiring neurotransmitter scheduled for only two outcomes, rather, two exits, one outcome. Mouth or ass, your choice. The cigarette.

The Warlock Sense of Humour

"Hello black oblivion, goodbye white hypnosis." The power had clicked off silent, so only silhouettes of gaping treelines defined the misty vacuum sites, negative spices, timed eternal so it seemed. Fortuitous, in a certain vein, moreso promontory, specifically disturbing in prophetic omen. When the power goes out and one considers the primal fear of being a youngster in the great unknown, you ironize the situation, laugh it off, and consider yourself the great holy warrior Arjuna, then, then, what dare from the darkness to disturb my waking volition. Thereby, excommunicating all unconscious drives of the fear factor until you are staring down at a butt end of a smoked complete cigarette, and thus, it comes down to, do you continue burning more death lights for pleasure and purposeful excursions to standing as solo light beams in towers of your own devisements, or do you return to the comforts of the nest, spark candles, or battery-infused screens to pass the time?

Mats needed to sleep more. Natural, time cycles, the plain sights of the limitless earth march. On such a night of specific silence, machinations deriving clear and capable what could be the ideal desires for the light, for consumption, for vocations to carry on in lonesome rides and quests for abstract fortunes, only gained by leap year lucks to catastrophic planes beyond a mere three dimensions, beyond mundane six senses, above and struck through the seven sins to salvation's lynchpin, the bottom line. Oh, yes, of course, it's all there, just waiting to be vested. So, now what? Security, taken care of, he should become a prep-advertiser, embrace the status quo, They're on the same team as

You, though that realization may be more conjuring to them than to you, tiddle-doo, all good fun. Mats was stoned.

The next morning, the notice for action arrived. Whereby, the observation of days mushed to the past two months was apparent and hence, bespoken, he was heir to numerous forays back to the social races. Clothes were delivered, suitable, pressed, zipped in body bags hung by deadwood waiting to be utilized for time-place specific functions for reputable agendas. Gorey did not even have to initiate personal addressments. It was all too obvious who really pushed the buttons and raised the levers to balloon-limitlike pressure. Gauged and motivated, Mats was, by now, on an overdose of indifference. Reaching the dream real is a twisted limbo, cogged into playing a buffoon role on a stage for capitalistic endeavor. You become the poster, or better yet, the reason for the poster, marked, trademarked, registered, protected, now, then just what? What? The key code, why, how, how is bullshit, but why and what, how do they dance around your spinning disorient specter? For no reason at all.

Mats was abashed at his uncanny predisposition to lose all inhibitions, now that he had been shackle free, commitment free, that he gravitated toward the subterfuge, the evisceration of guarantees and self-disposable bliss. He wanted to break the binds that had so eloquently curtailed his fortune, ever-booming, ever-growing, for holiday season was around, and Isos was the penultimate usurper of subscribers who sought subliminal bonds to ornate the feline orgasm to tidal waves of submission. Success was so smug.

Blind Vase Cleaner

The faces of the Damned. At prefabricated bases of influence, committed to show, on display, with facetious smiles, vapid stares, repose of status, prestige, farts. The face of the man coming off a mind bender, howling to the gorges he will never see, crying out for the satiation of bodily excretions, opining his place in the world as a fungible curse with problematic bottlenecks, hypnotizing himself to sleep in drink and acceptance by those incognizant to his petty digressions on an interior orchestra sympathetic to survival. All the granulations of such faces, prismatic at the helm of a gaudy chandelier hanging overhead waiting to fall on the predestined chump who will thereby be the martyr eschewed into place of memoir, commemorative to those who fought in such amoral clunkiness to get to a place to just say, Yes, I witnessed the spectacle firsthand, hell, I became part of the spectacle, and hell, I didn't even get much out of it, but the only way you could even suspect that was by the sacrifice in my face, the horror beneath, impenetrable, until you just know, from not only being there, but from knowing how to get there. Because hell, chance is a cruel cumb dumpster, and she only has laughs for you at the finish line.

Mats thought of Tara Thames and how it would work out better if he could erase his Isos, get off the junk pills, and go back to an anonymous potency that was his and his own, alone, private, safe, and away from these cast-offs of Hollywood-fantasy put on to pedestals of preoccupation, fortune, success. Suck me off and swallow more drinks before the great second bang comes to decimate this world order of disorder. So cheesy, so grainy, so dry, these bite-size treats to decadence, stare at the females, they make it tolerable, on a biological level.

The irony of the list was that it was two-pronged outcome contingent. You're on the list, you're damned. You're an anachronism. You stick out like a sore piggy tickled by luck and wipeout until you dissipate into a shade of any truth semblant from a corrupt experience. Might as well be on lithium and proclaim I'm one of those permanent traumas. I'm a self-made tragedy. People pay for me to be so. It's my burden and do I shirk the consequences. What's your name, do you have any dreams, maybe I can help, and you can help me sleep sound before the circus wakes up tomorrow.

Such melodrama disturbed Burlik, and thus, they ransacked off into a limousine in the night, skipped out on the awards for the campaigns of self-flagellating marketeers, commercial devils, and at the ripe dark hour 2:00 A.M., they were out on a field, lighting tiny beacons of Zen-inductive greenery, keeping them lit, superstitious to never tap down and kill the fire, shared, experienced, the same team flipping bird to the conventions that prude the senses. The fireworks were about ready set. The skies cleared of dilapidated waste via the spotlights a few football fields away. Big Hail Marys, at least four, to reach the rotunda of the death gathering. They'd light their fires and cause a conversant conversation. Just a byproduct of their own self-declaratory powers. We are rebels and we do not give a damn. Go listen to your mediocre music and your mediocre fashion sensibility and I'll see you at the next one, with some cocaine!

A great bonanza of light asphyxiated on the hydrogen-heavy sky, absent of naturals, saturated with artificial leakage from distant Hail Marys not breaching the proper thresholds, thus, secondary to the bonanza. The bonanza, first a great whirlpool, a great burst of fireball, a kaleidoscope of cataracts floating in lethargy. More, more, yes, more, don't stop. Until the meandering sirens breach the field, microphoned announcement, waves of recognition. See, if you look, we're in black-gown get-up, we have been there, we are a part of The Group, yes, Officer, thank you, we apologize for the embarrassment, we didn't mean to have to show you this is the way it is if you go this far down the rabbit hole, of a hell so preconceived as to overlook the Dantean specifics of serious circles. They're all muddled into one, the first ring, the outer ring, the one is of treachery, it's the first order, and see, we are the true guides, for if you seek entry into the nether realm of moral flipsides, you'll lose yourself in the moment and from then on, we can no longer Protect You.

They're gone, one more firework, cast the flames down onto the acacias, and bam, the department of Fire sets off a new circus act. Tax breakable, of course. Burlik and Odon gone, long gone, no need to witness the conflagration of creation, for now, it serves as a distracting entity, and absolute power can be achieved by commodity reassignment. See, the party host, the penumbra of petty shareholders, has an underlying operation underway, besought by Gorey as the lodestone of the entire Isos enterprise, as if it were, a Babushka doll, and at the center, the core doll under all the large more obnoxious layers, it'd be formulated in a true myopic wealth core. Hence, diamonds.

At the gate, scan the barcode, roll the windows casual, see, there was a fire, call your superiors if you doubt us (I know you won't), don't even mark it down, we need to do some damage control. You see the fear in his eyes for discovery and he resets back to his perch as the lone gatekeeper in the night, better left unchecked, he just wants his job and menial wage and return to the peace of his beautiful wife and ransack rampant offspring. What a better life, I'm serious, Burlik exclaims. Enough with your contemplations of the best, and who's better off, you're starting to sound like a liberal that discourages progress. Chuckles, parked out front, handicap. On camera.

On pick up, the packages already waiting at the interior guard gate, no one knows what it is. We're just transporters. A hightail chase of their own imaginations on the outset, skid out the pavement, leave some markings of conquering, and a cigarette butt just to say fuck your concrete, and back to the races, the great American race of motion and tide against the moon's running set. Are they even having fun anymore? Are they preprogrammed to be triggered by what they have been exposed to on an expository level of breakdown? What is really happening, why did they take these diamonds? What does Gorey really get from all this influence? Tools, levers, gauges, measuring rods, monitoring beams, lasered on the playground to come back to his mindwarping hands scurrying back and forth to create heat combustible until the great dissipation of the Agenda. The Agenda, whose Agenda? A piecemeal array of biological desires and logical needs in a capitalistic regime, so what, then what comes, the recycling of the desires until defense is outdated and archaic like shields against rockets. Oh, such profundity. Roadblock, better yet, rest stop. Flat tire.

The pallid steeple of the walls outlined the Hotel Grand against a backdrop of a dewy snow mountain curtain. Like a well-crafted cabinet containing shelves of trinkets, holy grails, and the occasional nook hidden within a shelf housing organic treasure, so it was the Hotel Grand, a meticulously constructed wedding cake on the Adirondack dough hoard. Here, a secret meeting was to be conducted, where briefing for missions concurrent on the acquisition of the diamonds was commensurate with the negation of certain predisposed commitments in order for the new developments to gain any momentum for new avenues of pursuit to be not only arrested for recalibration but also for new coordinates for disposal to be determined. Lots of confusion, lots of bullshit, Burlik and Mats were a day and night early. Hence, binge tactics.

The sun aflame with promises of what-if's and what-could-be's, the surf of the quiet falls miniaturized against the foreground of soothing lake containers, freezing to the frost surround, the rebel compatriots, stopping on a stony bridge overlooking the off-branch river downflowing to the below valleys, and the ominous motion of a golden eagle speedgliding across the grand panorama for cinematic pedant. At a more micro-level, the smoke being the foremost focus of the sight, all aforementioned as mere desktop sights for a splendid start to a lone day in lone country, free of commitments.

"What if we get snowed in?"

"I'll declare you a prophet and convert to your lifestyle."

"Like you already haven't psh."

"Hand me that squaw."

"Squaw?"

"Yes, squaw, good ol' chap."

"You're a true Englishman, now."

"Look, Mats. Don't give away your ignorance. It's too early for that."

Passenger Visions

Simple drives. Go green stop red. Yellow demonics. Laughing to the finish line, she said. He wished she said. It stuck like viral glue. The way the words melted off her glands muscled out by compulsive resonance. Rational, bubonic, at the heart of things preferably Unobserved, ignored, voided.

Lots of somber contemplation, fulcrum to hopeful gazes at the sublime bending of the contours. Silent, resolute, harrowing. See it for not had the bridge briefed a pause in the circuitry, Mats could excuse his conscious memory, to avoid the recall of the illustrious vignettes of driving in autos with opposite mediums. Their holes, his fantasy of their holes, his success rate in encountering the holes, now a mere dreamweaver on the still-clear windshields saving him from the momentous winds conjured by the curves in the road and the trees bordering with flexible shade and branch, and the pebbles gathering up the old rusted asphalt until dirt could carry on and erase the vestiges of man claiming this is his keep.

Such a daydream transpired on the road passage up the mountain to reach the hotel, and upon arrival, the ethereal feeling of gliding over scapes and meager sober thought processes took a backseat to the allure of the Maybe, the What If. Resolution should be set to expire on a date scheduled in the imminence, contingent upon Gorey, upon some other dissenters faithful and smart-laced, but for the binge to be a precursory refraction, there should be some strategic determinations confirmed by said driver Burlik. They needed a way out. It was around day 18 now, give or take, and with liberation from concrete text-written bounds, then racketeering was an inevitability, especially with so much insurance and nuisance derived from the insurance. Mats did not consider himself a ticking time bomb of chaos and changing wickers though he began to feel the insipid instinct to cover his back, guard his frontal, and beware the charlatans and mountebanks who arose with easy-to-implement answers and solutions to problems best framed as, well, when you put it like that ... I suppose this is the best course of action, given the dilemma. The dilemma was the rooms were not ready, though they folded this onto a tetherball of acting afoul at the front desk, whereby they were to take the grand suite, so as to replicate Gorey's authority, for they were the forerunners to the large party—booked, scheduled, organized, and with such a large bill due—they were treated with the utmost pomp and fortitude for any possible rude request they forsought to share with the adorning staff.

It was just loads on loads of liquor bottles and cigarettes, yet the manager still feared shenanigans were in store that could forecast possible damage and need for repair, decommission, of the rooms occupied, yet the ballroom was ready, and here, the débauche could be legendary and careless.

The way in *Giant* James Dean sabotages his own coronation at the grand opening of a hotel, so it was the role model for the play on habitats, pretentious performance art never self-aware, yet here they engaged the prostitutes. Wrong word, the willing conspirers. Finally taking advantage of the black book for one last hurrah, the digital path to flesh, and upon orgy, there was a standard need for refill and cohabituation, yet what was interesting most striking to Mats was the mobile nature of the ramrod of glistening legs exposed and willing. That they followed the drill, wherever it was going, and would show in upstanding fashion, readymade for entry, for courtship, for that death defying world of Fun, and come the sunshine, it'd be pleasantries in departures, for the continuation of the makeshift happenstance for Next Time, What If, yet to See, stare at the legs of Flight.

Look Bureaucrats

Akin to tardy school boys already under the influence before the crows come out for crumbs after morning breaks, Mats and Phillip stroll in to the conference arena, above the clouds, the mists waltzing over the lake and remnants of a quarry and a ravine of ravines shrugging against the mountainside dormant in magmas awake. Gorey petulant in disapproval, more disappointment, at what has come to his grand design and how its impersonable falter is so obvious to the company thereby.

It's all in the children, Gorey cries, beginning the monologue better summarized as follows the children cry, the children soldier onward, unbeknownst to what shall be around the blind curve in the paths divergent convergent upon moments of renown, before whence decisions must be determined and how to come to them, how to unite mind-body-spirit-soul, what can influence such predilections, predispositions to the folly, is order to take the reins, for the social contract, Rousseau and his demerits, or shall it be Lockean proto-cryptic Freudian whims that steal the cake, or the amalgam of all the bullshit spewed amongst the feral corridors of halls bespoken with locked microboxes with books scribbled and shared and abused, and wholesomely denounced, whereby they will be the seekers and redeemers of times better cast black along the horizon, at times when we, the determinate players, will be fading at medical clubs past our time in the sun, to pillage and forage and die peacefully, there's the rub.

Laughs, loud coughs, one of them even picked his nose and placed it under the table, a blown nose followed, a cigarette symphony, and to be honest, they began to look around at one another, eyes hitting visual contact with the other duets of soul, and maybe they had a cause on their backs, now they were just growing aware of the portent of such a notion.

The cadence of a man claiming responsibility, stewardship, requisite pomp and bombast for the horrors at work in the culture decline, the civilization crumble, the recompense for what to do about this and that sort of problem. A true Preterite, a true politician. Gorey, give what you are given, take everything as long as it is given in public, alms, charity, goodwill, moral symbolism via financial arms. See, at a time, Gorey had been quite the harlot of heroic endeavors, their coating sheathing him in a veneer like Olympian nectar, aristocratic prejudicial preference, mythic charisma, fear of his rejection on a social level. He had gravitas, oh, yes, he did. See, this was according to fathers and older brothers and elder cousins, and kinsmen of regimes long eradicated or absorbed or consolidated and now, in the new realm of time-given-space, he had a following, sure, but the self-aware indifferent diffidence showcased through the seeping eyes of drug-craving pseudo criminals crossed with semantical dissenters, educated and wealthy, what was the big ol' deal, just so as long they could carry themselves in a certain erasure of ideologies and institutions and memorize their experience as they underwent a conscious drive and journey to fuck the naysayers' women because those women want it the most, as soon as they are surely to admit it, given the right tonic, and screw the Montagues and Capulets of this world, so as long as they house and feed them, and like little rebels with tattoos at the new country club or the horse derby, they bespoke identity. Here and now, Gorey was rather demarcated a pedant, a speaker for appearance's sake, though they all were sure to admit, he had zealous pride and that sort of effect goes a longer way than the great white shark of hope already succumbing to never-giving-a-fuckness about living like hell, for what it was, what it is, is a neverending circle drain down the toilet to the pipeline of decadence.

"There's a price for decadence, sure," cried Gorey, this catching the table by a startling surprise. Is the old gabber onto the nouveau pastiche, is he reading the popular publications to get the proper terminology, pronounced so poignant, what a fuck word, almost shameful but so smiley, so smiley, so smiley. Now silence, stares, coughs, and one quick bid before transitioning to the apex of the death drive. Unity, peace, respect, all harbingers of nationalist enterprise propagandic and here we go, Gorey has a plan. We are to implement Isos part 2 point O and Mats, thank you, do you have anything to add. A silent No.

Make sure you all breed and have boys. Then, cycle them into packs, Boy Scouts, Eagles, Armies, here we go, and once they have that access point to followers, they can disseminate the true spoken word of God, these pamphlets will carry on, embedded in their words, their plays, their relationships. It's quite myopic, given that it capitulates, insidious overdrive, all through their mediums, mediums infinite. It's a curriculum hypnotique, in your packages, you will find a staunch course of feeding materials for the spawn. These children's books, these images, these films, especially those of the animated status, will resonate and serve as waypoints, catalysts for disarmament, rearmament, and waltz the sway of the regime until Revolution could be believed distinct, extinct, and dead, a magical myth of the way it was, even in the context of the given media circus, it will be Past, done, Over. So they will believe. Are you beginning to see the light, Youth of the Nation?

Fucking, fascist, mad in his methodology for stigmatizing mayhem. You had to give it to him, though, he could get a crowd going, especially of honest-able-bodied non-readers. He had a way with that high pitched hellcat of a voice that gargantuaned into a flurry of diminishing bellows followed by augmented hisses and arpeggiated solos of words so eloquent they do not sound complicated given the momentum and pace of mighty hopes and dreams to be realized in power plays of success, Goals, buzzers, sirens, Victorious!

At such a point, Mats cut Burlik off and seized the joint and said plain, "it doesn't even matter."

"But I want to know, tell me what he used to be like."

"The only predilection for your desire is arbitrary and insignificant."

"Wait until you go to sleep tonight, then we'll see what is important to you."

"Perverts anonymous."

"Look, it's not going to change, just harp back to some fantasy conception of the heroic guy before he gets hampered by the natural adversaries of the world, and gets a bit corrupt, a bit too inclined to drink the Kool Aid, to follow the schedule, to go along with the Order, you know, and what is spit on, a ramrod amalgam of something beyond tangibility or the opposite. A cipher that is more a glitch in the system, creating chaos and seizing order at seemingly happenstance events of instantaneous combustion or explosion, tidal in waves of Yes by God, you are someone who Understands, yes, yes, at other, No great Devil, you are so clouded in the shrouds of darkness down under the caves of the bottomless abyss. Be gone!

It's really a standard story, except, now, he wants us to Breed cattle and implant our Spawn to be little boys from Brazil, skewed to the Isos, drugged, programmed, ready for action, wherever it may be.

I even hear he has some investments in the cryogenics department.

It's beyond a department, it's a full R&D arm, multi-level.

Funny how fast people mobilize when it comes to money.

Bullrush the blitz, the big wave, they're all coming after you quarterback greenback surfer boy because when an opportunity coagulates into the pseudoevent for anticipatory damage control and preterite Fortune, Chaos can be spoiled to the Victors of Organized.

Civilization, oh that lovely Civilization."

"Well, get to the Gorey background, if it is so insignificant in the given context, yet now, let's come to a consensus. Let's get off the junk."

"Why, Mats?"

"It's the effects. They're quite subtle but they're skewing me deadly and trembling in the night, looming just beyond the black I can no longer see, there is something about it and what it is, only the independent entity the Isos capsule will be sure to know."

"We could ask the designers."

"They don't know, they, I mean, you, you're missing the point."

"Light up another one."

"So, you seek sabotage via saboteurs. Sabotage of the Saboteurs."

"Folding in on the regime we were so driven to be a part of and see it cultivated to empire and imperial spillage."

"Look, we were young, we won't become the same ciphers as Gorey."

"It's all given a context, a time, just when you're 50 years old, promise yourself, fuck what I care, just promise yourself, Don't you Dare Wear Makeup in Public."

"Only behind the lights, in front of cameras."

"Bingo."

The Money Behind the Magic Curtain

The going is tough, citizens of the State. The weather reflects morose kindred spirit, the folly of the fungible parts sebaceous and still-seizing the whining end of days. There's not much to goof on account of the order delineation, production capsizing and concurrent sell-offs with shark headed stupendous Ichabod Cranes scramming for cover.

Said the Slacking Cord, Robust in luck, you Devil

The milk and honey looked lurid. Staring at the mirror, focusing into the pupils, it gets weird, That's what Mats kept trying to put into structure, form, semantic cohesion. Not for long was his mind haunted by the shit storm of numbing sycophancy. Isos sedatives were gaining visual reference frames. It occurred to him that this could be taken two ways, one, immediate flight, successfully scared, cold straight and on the slow ride, hold back, let the hare win. The second way, to embrace the weirdness, had to be the way to go.

It wasn't so courageous, yet it was. What it was, to Mats, could be the summation of a man's fortitude. Sure the body is a beast to tame, but the mind, the mind has extensive bounds beyond history and tradition. The arena.

Of Uvula

It must have been six more months.

Expiration. Evisceration of the capital confines. Nevermore, innocence extinct.

The same pupils, yet they poached evanescent in amoebic definitions. Ill-kept facial hair prodding the borders like a garden forgotten. Through the bush, the blank gaze. The background noise, clear as chemically-treated water, minimal, grand merciful.

Aesthetics had been the primary goal, and upon achievement, credit the payout, the severance package, the continued inflationary doldrum of bonds junked, treasures without interest, equity without tax, Mats understood his benefit had a clear and tangible outcome. A pleasant home.

By the standards. By the eye. By universal aplomb. Order, precision.

Notice by mirror way, aft the shoulder, the cathedral of light rays breathing edges and contours to the cold, hard glass columns, descending in focus and size, an infinite reel. For he, too, caught in the meta-reflection, the mirror behind. To ramp up and down on the never-ending march, posed here and now, on legally deeded property.

Behold the Babylon that is yours, cerebrally yours, catered, a vast crater of prestige to solidify the state of affairs. You have made it, son. You have made it.

9 781944 527952